DEF

FC

TALES

DERRY

FOLK TALES

Madeline McCully (signature)

MADELINE McCULLY

FOREWORD BY
DR GEORGIA RHOADES

The
History
Press
Ireland

I dedicate this book to my grandchildren,
in the hope that they will cherish the wonder of childhood
and never grow too old to enjoy a good story.

First published 2015

The History Press Ireland
50 City Quay
Dublin 2
Ireland
www.thehistorypress.ie

British Library Cataloguing in Publication Data.
A catalogue record for this book is available from the British Library.

ISBN 978 1 84588 869 5

Typesetting and origination by The History Press

Printed and bound in Great Britain

CONTENTS

FOREWORD

I feel I have two homes, though I live in neither. One is Kentucky, which I left over 20 years ago. In a hollow near the house where I grew up, in the right conditions, you can hear a wagon and horses approaching from the top of the hill through the woods. They will pass right by the porch of the beautiful old house in the hollow, but you won't see them, only hear them. In the house, a starving woman goes through the cabinets in the kitchen at night, looking for bread. Those who live there will tell her to eat her fill, but she never is satisfied.

Some of these places were written about by Lynwood Montell in *Ghosts Along the Cumberland*, and for us that was a vindication of our history, that our stories had become larger than our small community, and that we were linked in that great web of folklore. Like Madeline, who has listened to storytellers and gathered a great collection of her own stories, I grew up with tales and myths told by old people. In my childhood, I saw butter churned and almost everyone I knew kept a cow or two, so such tales as 'Blinking the Cattle' and 'Blinking the Churn' are particularly evocative for me. My mother told me of smoke rising from most of the hollows when she was a girl in the 1920s, evidence of moonshine stills and our version of poteen. There were bullet holes in the door of the church, and a story to go with them; a tale of the dog nobody knew who came into a house to bite the son, who could not be cured by the madstone; and a story about two sisters who murdered their father one warm night. These stories may not have the grandeur of the skeleton on the Derry coat of arms or the patina of antiquity in Columba's exploits, but they do link Kentucky, which the Cherokee called 'the dark and bloody land', to the Irish and Scots who settled there and saw stories as a way to narrate who we are and why we are here.

The other place I feel at home is Derry, which I have been lucky to have visited more than twenty times. Through my writing, Derry's history has become even more important to me than Kentucky's. In preparation for writing my play *The Cook*, about the execution of Cecily Jackson at Bishop's Gate in 1725, I read the Bishop's diary, where he speaks of his fear of 'the murderous Rapparee', given life in this collection by Madeline. I was recently in the excellent Tower Museum, looking for context about Derry in the eighteenth century, and I will return to pay closer attention to Sir Cahir O'Doherty's sword, now that I know its story. Madeline also makes history alive in such stories as Amelia Earhart's and Denis O'Hempsey's.

What is heartening in all these accounts is how they link communities in our need to make meaning, to turn an event into a narrative. The story of 'The Waterside Ghost' resonates with what seems to have been a haunting at the house of Ann Haltridge in the Islandmagee legend I recently researched for a play I am writing. The story of Willie the fisherman fits with a wealth of Irish folklore about mermaids, from Lough Neagh's Liban to the mermaid who sits by Lough Derg, combing her hair. The white hare has a counterpoint in Scotland in the boasting of Isobel Gowdie and in Cornish stories of witches becoming hares, and the Feeny dragon recalls the Arbroath waterhorse who lurks beneath the kirk on the hill, waiting for the unwary who cross the bridge.

Those of us who have been able to hear Madeline tell stories will recognize her powerful voice in these tales and imagine that she is talking to us as we sit in a firelit circle. Her storytelling power is in evidence throughout the book, as in this creepy passage in which she prepares us to approach the place we will meet the Irish vampire: *A lone thorn tree would guide you to it but when you'd arrive you would see no grass or vegetation growing there and an enormous stone lies over the grave.*

Madeline's work in compiling these stories helps us know who we are and what we believe possible, or, for some, what we believe probable. In this collection, she honours folk wisdom and creativity, listeners and tellers, and the circle in which we sit together.

Dr Georgia Rhoades
Boone, North Carolina
July 2015

ACKNOWLEDGEMENTS

How can I begin to acknowledge the people who have contributed to these stories? Some are still alive while others have passed on and left a legacy of stories.

My thanks go firstly to my darling husband Thomas, who was forever supportive and encouraging. Thanks to the family for putting up with my absences (and absentmindedness).

Beth Amphlett of The History Press Ireland was a delight to work with and was considerate, approachable and ready to answer queries at all times.

I thank Margie Bernard of Derry Playhouse Writers who lovingly pushed me to write and Professor Georgia Rhoades who taught me to use those writing skills in her workshops.

I appreciated all the help given to me by Maura, Jane and Linda of the Derry Central Library and the staff of Shantallow Library, Mary, Emma, Diane and Marie-Elaine. They made research a pleasure.

I thank Jim McCallion of North West Regional College for his unfailing patience as he helped me improve my computer skills.

To all of those who shared stories, snippets and factual backup I want to say a big 'thank you'. Although I could not include all of the material, it is still floating around in my mind and will no doubt emerge in a storytelling session or two or maybe another volume.

Ken McCormack has a treasure trove of strange happenings and was always interested and interesting when I spoke to him. I want also to acknowledge Sean McMahon whose translation from Irish into English of *The Waterside Ghost* was begging to be included and I thank him for his permission to do so and hope that he forgives the slight meanderings from it.

I would like to mention those who reawakened my interest in folklore and who gave me a listening ear over the years, Liz Weir for her inspirational stories, the late Sheila Quigley who founded Foyle Yarnspinners and who was always so generous with her time, Bertie Bryce who taught me to 'recite' and Pat Mulkeen who was my 'Storytelling friend'.

Lastly I want to let my nurturers, Marilyn, Cora and Ellen, know how much I appreciated their listening and advice as I put this volume together.

INTRODUCTION

Most stories are unique to the person who tells them and although there are times when reason tells you that something could not have happened the way it was told, it is better just to listen and enjoy the moment. It is well known in Ireland that a wee bit of embellishment has made many a dull story better. The folklore of Ireland is littered with tales of taboos, fairies, superstitions, ghosts and banshees. The list is as endless as the Domesday Book but unfortunately many of our stories are being lost in this modern age when technology provides entertainment for the young and the not so young.

I am old enough and lucky enough to have experienced the 'big nights' or '*ceilidhe* nights'. Most summers until I was a teenager I went on holiday to my great-aunt's house in a rural part of Ireland. In those kinds of places people made their own entertainment; the fiddle and melodeon led the dancing and singing and as the night went on and the music stopped, it was then that the stories began. We youngsters opened the kitchen door a crack and listened to the big folk talk.

I heard many a story in my grandfather's house too, for he was a countryman who moved into the town. Looking back, the stories were told with such conviction and drama that I believed every one of them at the telling. The tales brought me into a realm beyond the ordinary with their use of rich language and the Gaelic construction of the sentences, for often, the people were barely a generation away from the Gaelic language itself.

One of the recurring things I remember as I look back nostalgically on those evenings is that stories were mainly told in the negative interrogative. It wasn't enough to say that I met someone on the way to the well, no, it was told in a much more engaging way.

'Didn't I decide to go to the well to fill the bucket and what d'ye think happened? Didn't I see wee Johnnie's Mickey walking down the road and him all of a fluster. Sure, did I not stop him and say tae him, "What ails ye?"' And so the story of a normal meeting became a tale, and we pulled our chairs closer to hear what the matter was with Johnnie's Mickey.

Most of the stories were about life around and about the district but on the occasions of ancient festivals like May Day, Lughnasa and the like, stories echoed the ancient ones. Samhain-Halloween was the time for ghost stories, and sometimes the listeners stayed in the house till daybreak for fear of meeting a ghostly spirit if they ventured out on the way home. If you believed it, the wee folk were more numerous than humans and were always a popular source of stories. There were stories of the colour red, hawthorn trees, fairies and iron, fairy pathways, the new moon, spilling salt, raths, standing stones and if you lived to be a hundred you would still discover more.

Many years ago, I interviewed three marvellous storytellers for the radio. They inspired me, and even though they have passed on, I remember them with gratitude and affection, they were Sheila Quigley, Bertie Bryce and Pat Mulkeen. We will never see the likes of them again.

The tales in this book are a selection of ones that I have heard, and others that I have researched, because my own versions have wandered far from the originals and I needed to pull them back. Most of them I have told in my storytelling evenings.

I hope you enjoy reading these as much as I have enjoyed writing them.

1

COLUMCILLE:
DOVE OF THE CHURCH
AND FOUNDER OF DERRY

It would be difficult to begin to write anything on the myths and legends of this city, without mentioning its founder Columba – Columcille. He is beloved by all and the people of Derry are rightly proud of him. His presence is remembered everywhere – in the street names, St Columb's Wells, Columba Terrace and Columcille Court; in the church names St Columb's Cathedral, St Columba's church, St Columb's church; in the naming of one of our most beautiful parks, St Columb's Park; and, endearingly, in the children's names, Colm and Columba. So it is fitting that this should be the first story in this book of the folktales of our city and county.

The city itself has been known variously as Daire Calgach, Doire Cholmcille, Derry/Londonderry and even recently as Legenderry.

Tradition suggests that Columcille was the founder of Derry (Anglicised from the Irish *Doire*, meaning Oak Grove) in August AD 546. Indeed there is a plaque on the wall of the side entrance of St Columba's church, Long Tower, in Derry that states this fact and inside on the main aisle a white marble stone is embedded which says:

+
SITE OF ALTAR
IN
ST. COLUMCILLE'S
DUBH-REGLES
546-1585

Columba

But there is one sure thing about Irish people and that is that they will always find something about which to disagree. And why not disagree about the site of Columba's monastery? There is a counter claim that his original church was founded where St Augustine's now stands, beside the Walls of Derry. All I can say is that people will believe what they want to believe and in Derry there is a saying, 'Why let the truth get in the way of a good story?'

To get back to Columcille, legend has it that he was born in Gartan in Donegal, then he became a student in the monastery at Glasnevin (now in Dublin) and when a terrible plague broke out, the abbot, fearful that his students might contract the Yellow Plague, sent them all back to their homes. It is said that Bishop Etchen of Clonfad ordained Columcille a priest and he made his way to Doire. There, the king offered him some land on which to build his monastery. Columcille refused it at first because he considered it heathen land but accepted it on the condition that he could set fire to it in order to exorcise the pagan ground.

Fire being fire and no respecter of boundaries, it began to creep towards the lovely forest of oaks that Columcille so loved, and the saint fell to his knees to pray that the oaks would be saved. He composed a prayer and, translated from the Latin, it is now known to be the beginning of the superstition that no man, woman or child in Derry would ever be killed by lightning:

> Father,
> Keep under the tempest and thunder,
> Lest we should be shattered by
> Thy lightning's shafts scattered.

Foolhardy young men have been known to run out into a lightning storm, shouting and challenging the lightning to strike. If it ever did, it has not been recorded.

There were also many superstitions about the destruction of oak trees. It was said that an important person who gave orders to have a tree chopped down for firewood died a horrible death and it was called 'A miracle of Columcille'.

Those who followed him attributed many miraculous cures to Columba, as he was also known, and legends and stories of a Guardian Angel were woven around him.

From Derry, Columba's light radiated to the far corners of the island, and tradition tells us that he was a great father of the church in Ireland, and that he ranks in importance with Patrick and Brigid. He was a man of learning, a scholar and a scribe, but he was more than that. Legend tells us that he was a son of the soil, born in the country and knowledgeable about country ways, a brother to ordinary men and women. He could cut turf, foot it and stack it, he sowed and harvested crops, fished in rivers, lakes and on the sea, gathered and dried seaweed. When he made mistakes he was open about them and used them to counsel the young.

One of the stories told about him was that as he was dressing he put on one sock and then a shoe, leaving one of his feet naked. Sure, wasn't that the very time that his enemies crept up on him and he had to run at a great disadvantage with one foot covered and one not? After that it was said that his curse would fall on anyone who dressed in that way. I have my doubts about that one, I must say.

Another curse attributed to him was that if you cut the last sod of turf, danger would follow you. And the origin of this story was that one day he was out at the turf bank, cutting away the sods with the slane and he had just cut the last sod when his enemies (it appears he had a lot of enemies) crept up from behind to attack him. He was unable to escape because, foolishly, he hadn't left a step up for himself. He'd cut the last step away like the others and he was stuck at the bottom of the bank at their mercy. Luckily, none decided to descend into the trench where Columba stood and they could not reach deep enough to wound him.

Wasn't he also seen as a prophet who could foretell the future? And there's quite a few who could quote his prophesies to you to this very day. Unfortunately, with the decline in the native Irish language many of those prophecies are lost or worse, they are of no interest to the present-day Irishman.

Of the stories of his departure from Ireland the one that is most quoted is that of the Brehon Law being invoked, and this is now considered to be the first law of copyright in history. It came about when he copied, without permission, a Latin Psalter that St Finnian of Moville had brought from Rome. When Finnian brought his complaint to the attention of Diarmaid, King of Ireland, the king gave his oft-quoted judgement; 'To every cow her calf, and to every book its copy.'

Columba, as we know from the stories, had a terrible temper, and when he heard this judgement his anger knew no bounds. He challenged Diarmaid to battle and as he made his way northwards he rallied the men of Ulster and Connacht behind him. At Cul Dreimnhe (Cooldrummon) in AD 561. Columba utterly defeated the king. But when he looked around the battlefield and saw the slain soldiers, bodies heaped upon bodies, he broke down and cried at the terrible loss of life. All told, it was about 13,000 dead, it is said.

In response, Diarmaid called the Synod of Teltown and, to Columba's great anguish, he was excommunicated, although this decision was later reversed.

But such was Columba's tortured spirit that he asked his friend from Glasnevin days, St Molaise, to impose a penance upon him. Molaise spoke to him and said that he must be the one to impose his own penance and it should be something very dear to his heart. Only that would bring him peace. Columba pondered on what might be his worst punishment and realised that it would be a fitting penance to leave his beloved Derry of the Oak Groves. So, although he was a stubborn and fiery man by nature, he was also an honourable one and so subjected himself to an exile where he would never again see his beautiful Ireland or step upon her soil.

Were all the tribute of Alba mine,
From its centre to its border,
I would prefer the site of one house
In the middle of fair Derry.

Columba sailed to Iona in a small currach in May AD 563. Before he left he stopped at a rock (now just below the Mercy Convent near Culmore) and took his last look at his beloved Derry. On that rock there are the deep marks of two footprints and one can see the city in the distance. At Shrove Head, the exit from Lough Foyle, he sang his farewell song;

> A grey eye looks back to Erin
> A grey eye full of tears.

Meanwhile, back in Ireland, the bards were gaining power, much to the concern of the chieftains, so in AD 575, Aedh, the High King of Ireland, called nobles, clerics, poets, storytellers and historians to a convention at the Hill of Mullagh. There he wanted to discuss and clarify and hopefully settle the matter of the power of the Irish bards in the Irish territory of Dalriada and the Scottish Kingdom of Dalriada.

St Columcille was invited to speak on behalf of the bards. It is easy to see how it was a dilemma for him because he had sworn never to see nor set foot on the soil of Ireland again. But legend tells us he found it difficult to refuse the bards. He solved the problem and salved his conscience by being blindfolded and by tying sods of Alba to his feet as he was led into the gathering. That very act made his word honourable and the Drumcait Convention, as it was later called, went down in history as a success.

An old story tells how Viking raiders desecrated Columcille's grave on Iona. They plundered all of the graves in the cemetery, searching for valuables, since it was the custom to bury items valued in life by the owner with them when they died. Columcille's coffin was made of fine oak and Mandan the Viking hoped that it would be lined with silver. Not being able to open it there and then, he brought it on board his ship, and when they were far out at sea he opened it. To his great disappointment there was no booty, only the beautifully preserved body of Columcille. In a fit of temper, Mandan closed the coffin and cast it into the sea, where a huge wave carried it away. Eventually, it was washed up on the

Irish shore and the peasants who found it brought it to the Abbot of Down. The abbot ordered it to be opened and to his wonder and delight he found that the treasure buried with Colmcille was, in fact, his writings. The abbot was in no doubt that this was the body of Columcille and he ordered it to be buried in the same tomb with St Patrick and St Brigid. This was done with the greatest fervour and reverence by the monks.

One of the clearest examples of the love of Columba for Derry, and the people of Derry's love for him, is the way he is remembered. On 9 June, his feast day, a congregation gathers at the Long Tower church and the bishop leads a service in the saint's honour, then a procession of men and women dressed in white robes walk to St Columb's Well where the water is blessed and ceremonially drunk. The people of Derry traditionally wear an oak leaf in their buttonholes in Columba's memory.

A stained-glass window on the left side of St Columba's church, Long Tower, bears the inscription of Columcille's own words,

> Crowded full of heaven's angels
> Is every leaf of the oaks of Derry.
>
> The reason I love Derry is,
> For its quietness, for its purity,
> And for its crowds of white angels
> From the one end to the other.
>
> My Derry, my little oak grove,
> My dwelling and my little cell;
> O eternal God, in heaven above
> Woe be to him who violates it.

DERRY'S COAT OF ARMS: THE STORY BEHIND THE SKELETON

The first question that visitors to Derry-Londonderry ask when they see the coat of arms is, 'Why is there a skeleton on it?' and that is usually followed by a second question, 'Who is it?'

Heraldry is history in symbol form and the past history of the area is emblazoned in the coat of arms of the city that joins the St George Cross and the sword of St Paul on the top half. The skeleton and the castle have been variously explained away and many stories have grown up around them.

Some say that the skeleton represents Sir Cahir O'Doherty who held the rank of chieftain of Inishowen from the age of ten all the way down to the reign of James I. He was slain at Doon, near Kilmacrennan, in Tír Chonnail on Holy Thursday in 1607. Others think that the skeleton refers to the starvation experienced during the famous siege of 1688 to 1689.

In fact, the skeleton and the castle quartered on the coat of arms refer to a much earlier date than either of these incidents. In 1305, Richard de Burgo, Earl of Ulster, sometimes referred to as the Red Earl, built Greencastle, which was at that time called Caisleannua, or the New Castle, near Mobyle, Moville. It was later called North Burgh by the Anglo-Normans. North Burgh was a very large building, and Edward Bruce held his court in it in 1316 when he acted as King of Ireland.

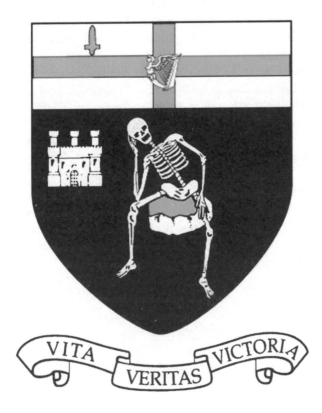

From 1310 to 1311, Edward II of England granted Derry-Columcille, Bothmean, Mobyle, (Moville) Fahanmure and portions of Inch to the Red Earl. He occupied this area until his death, when his son, the Dun Earl of Ulster, as he was called, then occupied it. But this Dun Earl had a bitter argument with his cousin Sir Walter de Burgo; it is thought that the argument was over a woman. The Dun Earl seized Walter in a skirmish at Iskeheen, and then imprisoned him in the dungeon where he starved him to death in 1332.

A mark or ring on one of the dungeon's pillars was supposed to have been made by the ring and chains that fettered him.

The daughter of the Red Earl, having been saved from drowning by this Walter de Burgo, attempted to carry food to him but, being detected, was hurled by her father from the castle walls and dashed to pieces.

The sister of Sir Walter de Burgo greatly resented what the Dun Earl had done to her brother, and encouraged her husband, De Maudeville, who owned extensive territory about Carrickfergus, to avenge her brother's death. De Maudeville with his men found their opportunity to kill the earl when he was crossing the ford at Belfast, returning from a hunting expedition in Ards in 1333, so his cruelty was avenged.

The death of the Earl of Ulster was the destruction of the Anglo-Norman power in the north of Ireland. The entire estate of the Earl of Ulster was returned to the King of England and remained with him until James I 'planted' Derry in 1607 and it was then that the new coat of arms was granted.

THE BORROWED LAKE

Long, long ago through the curtain of mist we call Time, there lived two sisters on the western edge of the island of Ireland. There was great jealousy in the oldest sister – some even claim that she was a witch but who is to know? The younger sister was sweet of temper and beautiful of face and loved her older sister. She could refuse her nothing and the witch played upon that loving nature.

Now, the land in the north around the older sister's abode became dried up and barren and nothing would grow for the sun had parched the land. An unusual happening in the island for this place knew much rain and wind that blew from the great ocean to the west.

The witch connived to get the beautiful lake that her young sister owned near the western shores. Oh, but she was a covetous one and no doubt.

She went to her sister and flattered her about her loveliness and how generous she was and how all the west looked up to her for her sweet nature. The young sister was so delighted that at last her sister seemed to show her affection that she blossomed. She grew even more lovely but didn't the older witch-like sister's heart grow darker and blacker and when she'd done enough of the flattery to ask for the lake she sidled up to the young girl one day and said, 'I would like to borrow your silver lake.'

'But it is the only water that I have,' answered the girl, 'how will I keep my land verdant and fruitful if I have not my lake?'

'I will return it to you on *Dia Luain* before the sun sets. Fear not, young sister, would you distrust me so?'

The girl thought for a moment, remembering how sweet her older sister had been recently, and she made up her mind to repay the kindness. She carefully rolled up the lake, but as she gave it to the witch-sister she pleaded, 'Be careful with my beautiful lough, its sparkle is precious to me. I will wait by the cliffs that fall into the great ocean until I see the ball of fire sink low in the sky. Return my lake on Dé Luain (Monday) before the sun disappears below the dark rim of the earth.'

'I will,' promised the witch, and rushed away with the precious lake under her arm.

As the sun began to fall in the sky on the evening of *Dé Luain* the young girl made her way to the high western cliffs and waited. The setting sun fell lower and lower in the sky and she began to feel anxious.

She called out, 'My sister, my sister, where are you?'

Just before the sun disappeared into the great darkness, her witch-sister came back empty-handed.

'Where is my beautiful lake?' cried the young girl. 'You promised to bring it back to me.'

'Alas,' said the witch; 'I promised to return it on *Dia Luain* [Judgement Day] not *Dé Luain* [Monday]'. It is you who have made the mistake, my dear sister.'

'Whatever you say to excuse it, you have broken your promise to me.'

'But promises are made to be broken, my sister. When I laid it like a carpet far to the north, in the in-between land it looked so beautiful. I could not bear to lift it.'

Her young sister's tears welled up in her eyes and made them shine as bright as the lake she had lost. As the tears ran down her cheeks she begged her sister to return the silver lake that she had borrowed. But, alas, she could not soften the heart of the witch.

And so the lake lay in all its splendour in the north and was given the name Lough Foyle which means the 'Borrowed Lake'.

On the western limit of the island there lies a barren place blanketed by crisscrossed rocks and beneath that heavy land lies the broken-hearted spirit of a trusting young girl.

FEABHAIL MIC LODAIN AND THE ORIGIN OF LOUGH FOYLE

If the story of 'the Borrowed Lake' isn't true then perhaps this one is.

Lough Foyle in the Irish language is *Loch Feabhail Mic Lodain* and that literally means 'The lough of Feabhail, son of Lodain.' Now, he was one of the semi-divine people, the Tuatha de Danaan who invaded Ireland, but his magical powers did not save him for he was drowned in the lough and his body was cast ashore.

How he drowned is a bit of a mystery, but the priest and historian Seathrún Céitinn, who lived in the seventeenth century, drew much of his historical knowledge from the *Annals of the Four Masters*, and in his book the *History of Ireland*, claimed that eighty-one years after the Tuatha landed on these shores, nine lakes erupted suddenly and burst over the land, and Lough Foyle happened to be one of them.

So the mystery of the origin of Lough Foyle remains. Was it named after Feabhail Mic Lodain who was unlucky enough to be drowned in the flood following the eruption, or did the witch who tricked her sister into parting with it steal it?

MANANNÁN
MAC LÍR

In the beginning, when Ireland was emerging from the invisible cloak of time, Manannán Mac Lír was a prince of the Tuatha de Danann, a race of supernaturally gifted people in Irish mythology. Sure, didn't he make places for all of the Tuatha to live in, for he was a responsible sort of being.

Now, after he'd done all that, he went away out of Ireland and it was said that he died in battle at Magh Cuilenn at the hands of Uillenn Faebarderg, a son of Finn. Well, didn't they bury him standing up on the Tonn Banks? And they lived to regret it, for a giant wave burst up from under his feet in the place known at the time as the Red Bog. And the brave Manannán rose again.

That lake got the name of Lough Foyle from one of the names of Manannán, and so it's been known ever since. And the brave Manannán was reincarnated as Manannán Mac Lír – the son of Lear – meaning the sea. But Manannán, being a decent sort, went around Ireland after that, doing bits and pieces of good in his own way. He enjoyed moving about, for he wasn't one to stay for any length of time in any place.

Well, listening to all the myths of the lough we hear that Manannán Mac Lír guarded the Foyle well. He had a mighty sword called Fragarach that was forged for him by the gods. Manannán wielded it well and it was said that you couldn't tell a lie or move with the sword at your throat and that's how it earned the name of 'The Answerer' or the 'The Retaliator'.

Now, this sword had some pedigree, and Manannán fought many battles with it before he passed this weapon on to Lugh, his foster son. Manannán was the one who rescued Lugh from the sea at Tory when his grandfather Balor ordered him to be drowned. You see, there was a prophesy from a druid that said Balor's grandson would kill him, so he decided that he would kill Lugh first. But Balor didn't know that Manannán had rescued Lugh, and didn't the very same Lugh kill Balor of the Evil Eye with the sword and fulfil the prophecy? Now, Balor and his shenanigans is another story for another time but let it be known that the evil man deserved it.

After that Lugh gave the sword to Cúchulainn, who later gave it to Conn of the Hundred Battles. That was some sword, wasn't it?

Sure this sword did other magical things for if you were the one using it, it placed the wind at your command, and it could cut through any shield or wall. And if you happened to be wounded by it, sure, you'd recover without a scratch or scar.

Some people still ask the question, 'Who was Manannán Mac Lír?'

Now there's a question, and all I can say is that he was changeable. He could be one thing one day and a different one the next. It depended on the mood he was in. You wouldn't know the likes of him, for wasn't he a god of disguise? He used these disguises to get his own way. One thing you can be certain of is that you don't want to get on the wrong side of him for 'tis a terrible temper he has when roused. All of us who live along Lough Foyle know that.

Manannán was a trickster and a magician, for couldn't he turn himself into a three-pronged wheel in order to travel faster across the land, and if that wasn't enough, didn't he have a magic boat known as Scuabtuinne, 'Wave-sweeper'? He could ride hell for leather over the waves and there was no escaping him if you were the one he was chasing.

He must have given his poor parents, Lír and Aoib, a wild time when he was young. Sure, there was nothing he loved more than leaping over the waves and riding his big horse, Enbarr of the Flowing Mane, across the sea until his hooves raised the waves thirty feet high and topped them with churning white foam. No wonder the poor sailors hated to see him coming, but sure, nothing his parents could do would stop him. He was a stubborn, impudent creature.

It was worse though, when he wrapped his invisible cloak around him and he would creep up unexpectedly and blow boats off-course and even sink some of them, for didn't he have his kingdom under the water at the mouth of the lough, just where the sand banks are? Many an unwary boat disappeared on those banks between Magilligan and Inistrahull when Manannán played God.

When he took the notion to catch a glimpse of his throne on the top of Barrule on the Isle of Man, the other part of his kingdom, sure, all he had to do was fill his lungs and blow and then he'd ride the towering waves. No wonder the locals along the lough would shake their heads and mutter, 'Manannán is angry today.' Sure, maybe he wasn't angry, just homesick, for as I said before, nobody likes to be stuck in the one place all the time and he probably missed his other wee island in the middle of the Irish Sea.

He wasn't invited too often to dine in any of the big palaces, but once or twice he invited himself. Needless to say, he always went in disguise. Sure, one time he heard that the chieftain, Aodh Dubh Ó Domhnaill, was having a big feast with musicians and all the local big-wigs and the bold Manannán dressed up as a bedraggled clown with water squelching in his shoes and a sword that was naked for the want of a sheath sticking out behind him. His ears stuck through an old cloak and he carried three blackened sticks of holly wood in his hand.

When Ó Domhnaill caught sight of him he wanted to know how such a dirty fellow entered his house and not one of the guards on the gate stopped him. Manannán spoke up for himself, and as boldly as you like, said, 'I can leave as easily as I came in and none shall stop me.' It was a bit of a challenge he was throwing down, just to see what Ó Domhnaill would do.

Just at that moment the musicians started to play and the clown covered his ears and shouted above them, 'By my word, Ó Domhnaill, that music is worse than the noise of hammers beating on iron. 'Twould deafen ye. Would ye stop your people making that racket?'

And with that he took a harp from one of the musicians and began to play on it, and right away there was total silence in the banqueting hall for there never was the likes of that music heard in all the land. It could have put a woman in labour or wounded men in battle to sleep.

Ó Domhnaill had a smile as wide as the ocean on his face, 'I have never heard better music than your own. It is a sweet player you are.'

'Oh,' answered the clown, 'one day I'm sweet and another day I'm sour.'

'Come sit at my table,' said Ó Domhnaill, and let me give you more fancy clothes.' But the clown would have none of it. So, afraid that he might leave, the Ó Domhnaill put twenty men to hold him and even more outside the gate and that brought the fiercest anger on the clown.

'Begod,' he said, "Tis not with you I'll be eating my supper tonight and if I find you giving one stir out of yourself or your big castle between this and morning I will knock you into a round lump on the ground.'

With that he took up the harp again and played music even sweeter, and when the whole gathering were listening he called out,' Here I'm coming, watch me well now or you will lose me.'

Sure, they didn't know that the clown was Manannán, and he swung his invisible cloak around him and disappeared. Now the men were all watching the gate with their axes lifted up to stop him leaving, but Manannán nipped each one and they swung around, thinking they were going to hit the clown, but instead they struck each other until they were all lying drenched in blood on the ground.

When they were all lying dead, the clown took the gatekeeper to one side and whispered, 'Let you ask for twenty cows and a hundred of the free lands of Ó Domhnaill as a fee for bringing his people back to life. Take this herb and rub it in the mouth of each man and he will rise up whole and well again.'

You might well ask why Manannán was so good to the gate-keeper. Sure, didn't he have a bit of sport and play with the mother before the child came into the world at all, and who is to say that he wasn't the gatekeeper's father? Anyway, that is how the gate-keeper got the cows and land from Ó Domhnaill and the men were grateful to be back in the land of the living again.

That was the sort of thing Manannán did for fun, and he was known to say that a life without humour is like a tree without leaves or a spring without water.

Manannán was always up to something when he wasn't chasing the women, for, as you've probably gathered, he was a wild man with the ladies and always had a great liking for them. But not everything went his way for he never got the woman that he coveted above all others – the Princess Túaige.

It might surprise you to know that Manannán had a wife by the name of Fand and she was a goddess in her own right, but sure, they had an argument and three demons attacked her kingdom. And 'tis here that the brave Cúchulainn enters the picture for sure, didn't he take Fand as his mistress and him had a wife of his own?

Now, when Cúchulainn's wife, Emer, heard this didn't she come after him? And Fand was looking for a way to escape Emer when she saw her own husband Manannán appearing in a 'magic mist', so she cleared away off back with him. Begod, it came as a great surprise that he took her back, for he wasn't known to be a for-giving god. But then, she was a bit of a poet and used it as a bit of flattery:

> When Manannán the great married me
> I was a wife worthy of him.
> A wristband of doubly tested gold
> He gave me as the price of my blushes …

So just in case Cúchulainn would follow her, didn't Manannán shake his cloak of invisibility between her and him so they might never meet again in time. And what did poor Cúchulainn do but take a draught of forgetfulness to ease his heartache at losing Fand.

It's a pity when they were burying Manannán that they didn't bury him horizontal, for if you were a God, being buried upright meant that you could face and vanquish your enemies. Maybe that's why the Tonn Banks are so beset by angry waves that they form one part of a triad known as 'The Three Waves of Erin'. Many shipwrecks have occurred there, and the spirit of Manannán still rides on the storm, wearing his invisible cloak. I haven't seen him myself but sure, you wouldn't catch me on a boat anywhere near the Tonns.

THE DEATH OF PRINCESS TÚAIGE – THE GODDESS OF THE DAWN

In earlier times the River Bann estuary was called Túag Inbher and this strange name was derived from a maiden who was beautiful beyond compare. Túaige was known as the goddess of the dawn and was the daughter of Conall Collamair.

It was her misfortune to catch the eye and attention of the great sea god of Lough Foyle, Manannán Mac Lír. Manannán was used to getting his own way, for if he didn't, he simply used his magic. Once he laid eyes on Princess Túaige he lusted after her. His heart was filled with desire and he coveted her as he had never coveted any woman before. He made up his mind that he would get her one way or the other.

He watched her secretly as she swam in the waters that flowed from the mountains of Mourne, *na Beanna Boirche,* through the great Lough Neagh, *Loch nEachach.* Sure, she sang as she emerged from the depths of the water and such was the sweetness of her voice that anyone hearing it was greatly enchanted. Then, one day Manannán went back, but there was no sign of her. She had gone from that place. The son and lord of the sea could not rest, so smitten was he. He ordered his druid, Tara, to follow her and find out where she lived and to report back to him.

For months the druid searched and waited but no sign did he see of her. Manannán was becoming very angry and frustrated and

sent word to Tara that great misfortune would befall him if he did
not find and lure the beautiful girl to Lough Foyle. Tara redoubled
his efforts, mesmerising the fish of the sea to help him, and eventually he found her, but she was unwilling to follow him.

Faith, Manannán had a hard time controlling his anger with
the druid and his passion for Princess Túaige so he tried a different
tack altogether. He sent his musician, Fear Fe MacEogabail, who,
by the way, had a magic touch with the music, to entice her to
the mouth of Lough Foyle where he, Manannán, would make her
his queen in the Otherworld-under-the-Waves. He dressed poor
wee MacEogabail up as a maiden and that was a crafty move, for
Princess Túaige would not expect any conniving from another
woman. Indeed not.

When the Fear Fe started his slow rhythm, it cast a spell on
the lovely princess so that she fell into a deep sleep on the sand,
enchanted as she was by his music. Fear Fe tried to lift her but
although she was a lovely young woman she was well toned from
all that swimming and a bit of a weight for a wee man. He knew
that he couldn't carry the princess as far as the Bann mouth by
himself. He was in a flummox asking himself, 'What am I to do?'

There he was, standing on the shore, looking for a washed-up
branch of a tree or something of that nature that he could put
Princess Túaige on and drag her along the coast to Manannán. It was
the only solution he could think of for a man of his small stature.

He had no sooner turned his back than a huge wave swept up
out of nowhere and carried the princess away. She was drowned,
without a doubt, for no one could survive a giant wave like that.
Fear Fe knew right away that he would be killed stone dead by
Manannán and the poor fellow tried to swim after her. But the
current was that strong that he got nowhere fast and landed back
on the shore. That wave that took the princess is called to this day
the Tonn Túaige, and is one of the three sorrowful waves of Ireland.

Fear Fe lamented Princess Túaige's death, for he knew that his
own might follow in a short time after he told Manannán. So,
in the vain hope that he could still find her miraculously alive
he searched in every secret place along the estuary but eventually,

he made his fearful way back to Manannán. He had to admit that Túaige had been unable to save herself because of the slumber spell he had cast upon her with his music. The son of the sea smote him with a mighty blow and killed him.

On a stormy night the roar of the waves which break over the Tonns is said to foretell a great calamity. In mythical times it could even tell the death of a king.

There are three magical waves in Ireland: Tonn Chliodhna, in Glandore Harbour, County Cork; Tonn Rudraige in Dundrum Bay, County Down; and Tonn Túaige in County Derry.

Some archeologists believe that the first-century Broighter gold hoard discovered in 1896 may have been part of a votive offering to the sea god and that the miniature gold sailing boat was in memory of the death of Túaige. The spot where the gold was found was reclaimed land on Lough Foyle's foreshore and might well have been where the ancient peoples came to appease the anger of Manannán.

WHITE HUGH (AED) AND THE ROUT OF THE VIKINGS

In AD 795 the first Vikings came across the sea from Norway and Denmark and began their pillaging of Ireland. They were a crafty enough race, for once they defeated the native Irish they established settlements and mingled with them by marrying the women and having families. They reserved their raiding for the unconquered areas. Even after their battles they were beset by insurgents among the natives for, needless to say, the Irish clans were not of a mind to be overthrown by foreigners.

Lough Feabhail, as Lough Foyle was known then, was very attractive to the Vikings. It was an excellent harbour, narrow at the mouth and widening out towards the modern-day Derry, and from there they could raid north, south, east or west. They established a large settlement on the banks of the lough but they didn't go unchallenged. Niall Caille, of the Callan, fought them off near what are now Londonderry and St Johnston. The Annals of Ulster record that Niall 'routed the foreigners in Daire Calgaig, Derry, in AD 833.' In that year he became the High King and he wasted no time asserting his kingship. In AD 845 he fought the Viking 'heathens' once again and routed them at Mag Ítha, St Johnston.

Now, on the death of Niall in 866, his son Aed (Hugh) was elevated from King of Aileach to High King of Ireland and the reins of power were passed to him. He wasted no time and set off around the north coast of Ireland, attacking the forts and settlements of the Vikings. *The Annals of the Four Masters* tells us that White Hugh gathered his allies to 'plunder the fortresses of the foreigners, wherever they were in the North, both in Cinel Eoghain (modern Londonderry, Tyrone and Donegal) and Dal Araidhe, (Dalriada) and he carried off their cattle and accoutrements, their goods and chattels.'

In *The Annals of both Ulster and Ireland*, a clear account is given. They tell us that 'Aed [Hugh] son of Niall inflicted a great rout on the Norse-Irish in Glenn Foichle and a vast number of them were slaughtered by him.' *The Irish Annals* also say that Hugh 'defeated them, and slaughtered the Gall-Gaedil, and brought many heads away with him.'

When he returned to Grianán of Aileach he knew that he was in an enviable position for the fort stood on the crest of a high hill from which he had a clear vantage point. He could see as far as Lough Foyle to the east and Lough Swilly to the west. White Hugh was determined to finish the Vikings once and for all. He was confident of victory for hadn't he fought the deadly battle with them before at Glenn Foichle?

The Annals of the Four Masters tell the story:

The foreigners of the province came together at Loch Feabhail Mic Lodain [Lough Foyle]. After Aedh [Hugh], King of Ireland, had learned that this gathering of strangers was on the borders of his country, he was not negligent in attending to them, for he marched towards them with all his forces; and a battle was fought fiercely and spiritedly on both sides between them.

The victory was gained over the foreigners, and a slaughter was made of them. Their heads were collected to one place, in presence of the king; and twelve score heads were reckoned before him, which was the number slain by him in that battle, besides the numbers of them who were wounded and carried off by him in the agonies of death, and who died of their wounds some time afterwards.

The gory battle that ensued has gone down in history as one of the
bloodiest battles ever fought on Irish soil. Hugh and his men rampaged among the Vikings and slaughtered them with little heed or
mercy and it was said that the waters of the estuary were stained
red with the blood of the foreigners. So much so, that the Ulster
was free of the Viking presence for many years.

It is not known how many of White Hugh's men were killed in
the battle but at least 240 Vikings met their gruesome end there
and Hugh's men, on his orders, severed heads from the bodies
of their enemies. 'He gained a victory over them at Loch Febail
(Lough Foyle) and twelve score heads taken thereby.'

But the Vikings were persistent in their bid to conquer and
settle, and in AD 919 thirty-two ships sailed up Lough Foyle under
the command of their chief, Olbh, who by all accounts was such a

fearsome character that even his own warriors were afraid of him. On Olbh's command they plundered and killed all in their path.

'Three hundred of the Cinel-Eoghain and foreigners were slain, together with Maelruanaidh, son of Flann, heir apparent of the North,' according to the Four Masters. Meanwhile Black-Kneed, Niall's son, Muircertach, grandson of Niall Caille, from his base at Grianán of Aileach, won a number of victories over the Vikings at Strangford in AD 926 and in Dublin in AD 939. After he died in AD 941 it would take another seventy years and the final Battle of Clontarf in AD 1014 for the Viking age to end.

It took a century and a half after White Hugh came down from Grianán to fight the Battle of Lough Foyle for the battles and power-seeking to finally come to an end.

We have to ask the question, 'Did we learn anything from history?'

THE MERMAID OF LOUGH FOYLE

*I'm not sure where I heard this story first but I know that my father
heard it from a fisherman in Lough Foyle. Mermaids are often
referred to in Irish folk tales, and songs abound with the theme.*

Willie was a fisherman who lived along the northern seafront, just
beyond Magilligan. When the weather and the tides were right he
gathered dulse (edible seaweed) to supplement his fishing. He was
not averse to taking a stroll along the water's edge of a morning, for
it cleared his head. You see, each night he usually tried two or three
sips or more of the poteen that he brewed on the hill still – just to
test it, you understand. If anyone knows what poteen does to the
mind then you'll know why he needed a wee walk in the fresh air
every morning. Poor Willie was a lonely man with neither wife nor
chick nor child and sure nobody begrudged him his 'wee drop'.

Well, on this morning, the loveliest spring morning, didn't he
see something moving on the rocks away up at the far end of the
beach. He wasn't of a mind to walk that far but there was something that looked a bit strange about the thing. It didn't look like
a basking seal or anything that he could think of, so on he walked
for a wee 'nosey'.

He was thinking to himself, 'If it isn't a seal what is it?'

Anyway, not wishing to frighten it off by clattering over the
pebbles, he slipped down to the sandy strip beyond the sea wrack.

When he moved closer he got the shock of his life because there, sitting on the rocks, looking at her reflection in a rock pool and combing her hair, was a gorgeous girl. She hummed as she combed and Willie, right then and there, fell madly in love. Willie, who was wont to believe that love had passed him by, just stood there watching, unable to do anything but look. He scarcely dared to breathe. The poor man's mind was in a dither.

Oh, but she looked graceful and beautiful and was so totally unaware of his admiring glance that he was just entranced. It was only when she finished combing her hair and bent down to look into the pool that he realised he was beholding a mermaid, for it was then that he saw her fish tail, bright turquoise, silver and green, shimmering against the dark rock.

Now, that caused Willie to think very quickly, because he'd heard of mermaids from his mother when he was just a lad. He racked his brains as he tried to recall what he knew about them.

Only one fact was clear in his mind and this was it: if he could touch her tail she would be his, for she would forget she ever was a creature of the sea. He took off his shoes and crept towards her, but when he stepped on a sharp rock, sure, didn't he let out a stream of words that his mammy would not have liked to hear, God rest her soul. And wouldn't you know, at the sound the mermaid turned and her big ultramarine blue eyes opened wide when she saw Willie. She tried to clamber off the rock, forgetting that the tide had gone out and she was stranded. Ah, the poor wee thing struggled clumsily to pull herself over the sand, but Willie was quicker. He stretched out his hands and the tail slid off her, clean as a whistle. Willie shoved it into his deep pocket, making sure she wouldn't touch it, for if she did wouldn't she turn into a mermaid again?

From that second on the mermaid had no recollection of who or what she truly was. She looked and acted like a human girl, although she was far more beautiful than any girl Willie had ever seen.

Didn't Willie bring her home and when he had her settled in his house he hid her tail in an old, dry drain behind the back wall. When he went back into the house she was walking around, touching everything and sure, Willie felt a bit embarrassed because there

was a layer of dust as thick as a slice of soda bread on the dresser
and the floor hadn't been washed for six months or more.

The mermaid didn't seem to notice, so he sat her at the table
and made a big pot of tea that she didn't seem to like. He dipped

a cup in the bucket of fresh well water and she gulped that down and smiled and sure, didn't Willie's heart melt again when he looked at her?

'Now,' he said, 'we'll have to give you a name. How about Mara?' She repeated the name several times and seemed delighted with it, so with great ceremony Willie bestowed it on her by touching her head. All that evening she kept repeating it, to Willie's amusement.

Over the next few weeks, Willie fell more and more in love with Mara and she with him, but, like all country places, there was some talk in the village when Willie didn't turn up to the pub for several evenings. A couple of his friends decided to call on him, and when they arrived and looked through the window, there in the kitchen sat Mara, looking as beautiful and content as could be, with Willie beside her and the two of them canoodling.

They rushed off, thinking it best to tell the minister what they'd seen so he could handle the affair, but it was hard for them to contain their curiosity, so they stopped off at the pub and told the world and his mother about Willie's new girlfriend. When the minister set off the next day to see Willie they followed him.

Now this minister was young and fairly new at the job, and he was determined that there wouldn't be talk in the village about Willie living in sin, so he would make sure that they would tie the knot and be married in God's presence or he would have to give up the ministry altogether.

When Willie explained about Mara being a mermaid he thought that Willie was being a bit of a take-a-hand, trying to fool him just because he was green around the ears, but Willie was so sincere in his protests that the cleric had to believe him. Now, that left the poor man in a predicament. His training hadn't covered marrying mortals to mermaids but rather than have a scandal in the village, and putting his theological doubts aside about the validity of such a service, he decided to perform the marriage. He was of the opinion that the bishop might not believe Willie's story if he should hear about it and since he, the minister, was the one faced by the determination on Willie's face, he went ahead and married them.

The drinking companions peeking through the window couldn't wait to spread the news far and wide, and there was a goodly amount of gossip. The women all asked the same question: 'Why did such a beautiful girl agree to be married to an auld crank of a man?' But Mara seemed perfectly happy, and soon Willie's story faded from the village gossip.

Well, the pair lived for years in tranquillity and peace. Mara became a very efficient housewife and was popular among the neighbours, for she was willing to help at any time. Three children were born in due course, two boys and a girl, and Willie was a happy man. But that was all soon to change and drink was the cause of it.

You see, Willie regularly put up a wee still for poteen making but he was watchful of the danger of the 'revenue men'. One evening one of the children came running shouting, 'Da! Da! The Revenue man is coming up the lane.'

Willie jumped sky high and pushed the piece of apparatus called the worm into the same dry drain as his wife's tail, and there it stayed for several months until Christmas, when Willie decided to make his seasonal 'wee run of poteen'. He sent Mara out for the worm, telling her where it was hidden, completely forgetting that many years ago he had placed her tail there.

As Mara reached into the drain for the worm what did she feel but her tail! It was as if she'd suffered an electric shock. Her hand closed around it and she pulled it out. There it was, glittering silver, turquoise and green. Her eyes turned to ultramarine and she felt the call of the sea in her body. Once reunited with her tail again she reverted to a mermaid on the instant. Willie, her children, and the poteen were immediately forgotten.

The sea was only a bare few yards away, and she hastened towards it like the wind and jumped in. Some people say that she was never heard of again but that is not the end of the story.

Strange things happened to the family. The two boys grew into men, the sea was in their bones and they sailed the north coast of Ireland fishing, until one day they did not return home. Two days later, beyond Rathlin Island their boat was found filled with fish, but there was no sign of them. Just like their mother, never again were they seen.

Willie's daughter often wandered along the shores, listening to the sound of the wailing wind and the roar of the waves. She told Willie that she heard her mother and her brothers' voices in the wind, calling to her. Willie was afraid that people might believe that she was crazy so they lived a quiet life with Willie keeping a close eye on her. But it was no surprise to Willie when she too disappeared into the ocean, never to be seen again.

Willie didn't last long after that, and when he was dying he asked the minister to make sure that he was buried near the sea. The strangest part of the story is that a spring tide rose higher than ever before that year and eroded the land beyond the shore, and would you believe that it washed away the part where Willie was buried?

If the locals heard the stories going around about Willie and the mermaid they didn't comment, and who are we to say what really happened?

9

CUIL, THE MAN WHO MADE THE FIRST HARP

Long after the great St Patrick came to Ireland there was a man who went by the name of Cuil. And in case you're thinking that he was related to the giant Fionn MacCumhaill I could tell you now he was not, for this man wasn't of any high stature. In fact, he didn't stand very high at all. He was a bit smaller than his wife, and to prove it she was called Canoclacht Mhór, which, as you know, means Big Canoclacht. And the thing about her was that she had a voice and a temper to match her size. Sure, she had the devil of a tongue, which could no more say anything good than she could stop breathing, and when she wanted poor Cuil to do anything he jumped to it like an ant on a hot piece of turf. When she suggested going to the shore at Inver Túaige, as the Bann Mouth was called then, he jumped to it and they went, and him carrying all her necessities for the shore.

Well, as soon as they arrived there she sat herself down and very soon, what with the fresh air and the soothing sounds of the waves, and the sweetest voice of the wind, didn't she fall asleep? And as for him, he began to enjoy the first bit of peace and quiet that he'd had for a long while.

'Oh' he thought, 'life would be wonderful if only I could have this every day, her voice stilled and me just able to relax.' Sure, so at ease was he that he began to feel drowsy, and who could blame him?

He was sitting on the shore, his back against a rock, and slipping into such a slumbersome frame of mind that he nearly fell asleep. And it was then that he began to listen to the sweet music that the wind was making when it played through the skeleton of a big whale that had washed up on the shore.

Cuil was a bit of a thinker, for a man needs to do something to tune himself off from an obstreperous woman like Canoclacht Mhór. When she began her ranting and raving Cuil went off to a different place in his mind. Wasn't that the best way to deal with the burden of a whining wife, to go into his own wee world?

And wasn't this music of the wind something to think about? Sure, it would give him peace if he could make something that would put her to sleep when she was of a mind to scunner him with her tantrums.

There was a lump of a tree lying beside the whale's skeleton, and he began hoking and poking at it with his knife. Even before Canoclacht Mhór woke up, he managed to make a shape just like the bones of the whale and put strings on it with fish gut. At first, when he began to play it sounded like a shoal of harpies coming in from the North Sea and it woke his wife. Sure, she raised hell at being so rudely wakened and she battered him over the head. But, despite her angry words, he carried the rough instrument home, and over the next few days he perfected it, and wasn't the music as sweet as a baby's smile?

That night he sneaked it into the house and when he saw the tantrum beginning to settle on Canoclacht Mhór he took out his 'harp', for that's what he called it (after the first sounds that he produced), and began to play. He closed his eyes, not wanting to let his wife guess his intentions, and the music flowed out. When he heard the wee snores from his wife he opened one eye and then the other and begod, there she was in front of him. Asleep!

And from that day till the day he died he never had a bit of trouble with Canoclacht Mhór, for whenever she started her ranting, out would come his harp and he let the music lull her into a deep sleep.

And that was how the first harp came to be made and all because of a bad-tempered wife.

When the word went around about this new thing that had a lovely sound, sure, everybody with a wee bit of music in their souls wanted one, and over the years the bards took it on and it enjoyed a great reputation.

Long after that, one of the bards who lived in Magilligan, not too far away as the crow flies, went by the name of Dennis O'Hempsey. Sure, Dennis would be known as one of the greatest harpers who ever lived. Some would say as good as O'Carolan himself. And it all went back to Cuil and the music from the whale's skeleton.

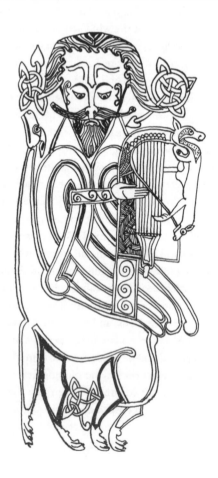

10

BLACK SATURDAY ON THE TONN BANKS

Now, many a tale was told around the hearth that hadn't its feet on the truth but there's many a strange tale told of the sea around Ireland that are true, and far be it from us to dismiss them. If we don't learn from them then we can suffer the consequences with our own foolish behaviour later on.

The fishermen on the Foyle estuary know this to their peril, for many have disappeared when Manannán, the sea god, was angry enough to swell the waves and pull their ships down to his underwater kingdom.

Now, I'm telling this story and you'll hear it over and over again for it happened over a hundred and fifty years ago when a fleet of fishing boats set sail from Magilligan. It was a calm enough Saturday in the month of November when they cast off and headed towards the Tonn Banks that lie between Inistrahull and Magilligan, at the mouth of Lough Foyle. We all know that the Tonn Banks are very dangerous at the best of times but even more dangerous for the unwary when the weather turns from calm to storm, and that can happen in a matter of minutes.

It is well known that many ships passing by on their way to or from Derry have been wrecked there, and it's a wise sailor who will avoid the Tonns if he has to sail further upstream from the North Sea to Derry or beyond.

The local fishermen are well aware that it is an area to be avoided, but sometimes familiarity leads to carelessness and carelessness leads to disaster, as happened on that fateful November day all those years ago. When the boats set off from the shore the men were all in fine fettle, it being the calm day that was in it. Still, these fishermen should have known that the sea could be as cantankerous as a cruel mistress who has her tantrums when and wherever she likes.

On this day she chose her time well, for she waited till the boats were just far enough out from land to assail them with a hurricane. It started off with a whistling of the wind, and the sails filled so quickly that the boats sped faster than the fishermen expected, and it was no time until they were nearly upon the treacherous banks. The wind changed to a gale and the lookout on the lead boat swore that he saw Manannán gallop towards the boats on his fearsome horse, scattering the white tips of the waves before him. Then the first wave rose and crashed over their bows and the fishermen knew that they had a very angry mistress or sea god on their hands. They tried hard to keep the boats facing into the waves, but they couldn't succeed every time, and one by one, each turned sideways, overturned and sank. The men were thrown into the sea and, as was the tradition in those days, few of the fishermen had ever learnt to swim. There was a superstition among them that if the sea wants you she will get you and 'tis better to go quickly than to struggle.

One man, however, did not let go. William Magenniss grabbed an oar and held on, for he was newly married and had a child on the way and that child would not grow up fatherless if he could help it. He clung on for dear life and kicked and paddled until he was able to reach the shore. By the time he crawled out of the water he was almost dead.

When he finally had the strength to raise himself from the sand, freezing cold and exhausted, he was confronted by a sight he did not expect to see. There, on the banks, he saw his companions walking along with folded arms as happily unconcerned as you like. Nothing could express the joy he felt that they too had survived. He shook his head and got to his feet, intending to join them, but when he called out they disappeared like the mist. When he looked back to the sea it was as calm as could be, not the tiniest wave in sight nor the sound of the wind to be heard.

What could he believe but that his friends were not drowned but taken off by the inhabitants of the Enchanted Castle? He turned around again and gazed out to sea, but saw only the barren banks.

When he was rescued and brought to land there were sixty-five widows waiting on the shore. He related what he had seen, and many a widow believed him but many did not.

That day became known as Black Saturday.

11

THE LEGEND OF ABHARTACH, THE IRISH VAMPIRE

Long, long ago, the chieftains in Ireland fought against each other their whole lives and there was much bad blood. They fought over what god was best, they fought over the best land, and they even had mighty wars over women. In fact, there were very few things that they didn't have a skirmish or a war over. But when the following tale was told by the bards to the chieftains of Ulster they all came to the same conclusion when they heard it, that there are evil beings around and they have 'the Bad Blood'.

Now if 'bad blood' is translated into Irish it becomes *'droch fhola'* and it is pronounced drocula, which is but a hair's breath away from Dracula. You can ask yourself if it's possible that Bram Stoker, who studied in Ireland, might have heard the legend of Abhartach and that this inspired him to write his story of Dracula.

It was well known in the country around Glenuilin, the glen of the eagle, in an isolated and remote townland in County Derry called Slaghtaverty, that there was a monument described as Abhartach's Sepulchre, although the people around call it the Giant's Cave. A lone thorn tree would guide you to it, but when you'd arrive you would see that no grass or vegetation grew there and an enormous heavy stone lay over the grave. If you happened to pass by you would be wanting to know who or what was Abhartach, and here's the story you would hear from the locals.

Legend says that in the fifth century there was a poet who had a son whom he called Abhartach. That was a nickname for a dwarf because that's what the child was, and it comes from the Irish, *Abhac*. But wouldn't you think that the son of a poet would be a kind and gentle creature? Well, you'd be wrong about this one for he was a brutal warlord who lived in a hill fort, and from there he went out to petrify his people. So evil was he that his terrified subjects got rid of him, but sure didn't he come back to wreck havoc and vengeance among them?

Some say that he was a wizard, a magician and a villain, but he was more than that, for although he was dwarfish in stature it didn't stop him being one of the most cruel beings ever encountered in this land. People were scared witless of meeting this strange, wee man on the road or in the fields, for, being a magician, he could turn himself into any sort of an animal and could even become invisible if he had a mind to. Many a one hearing a strange noise turned around and found he'd appeared out of nowhere, and he didn't hesitate to beat the life out of anyone who got in his way. Even after death no corpse was safe, because it was rumoured that he sucked the blood out of his victims and flung their bodies over his shoulder and fed them to the wolves, his only friends.

People tried to give him a wide berth as he ran amuck around the countryside on his vengeful rampage, usually under the cover of darkness. But eventually everyone meets their match and that match was a neighbouring chieftain by the name of Cathán, who was persuaded to do the deed for them. They wanted him to kill and bury Abhartach to rid their countryside of his evil presence. Cathán considered himself strong enough and fit enough to slay Abhartach, and he was fed up with the stories of the blood-sucking dwarf and the tales of his acts of cruelty on the innocent people of Slaghtaverty and the district about there.

Cathán was smart as well as strong, and he found out the place where this monster had his den. One night, when the moon was hidden behind the clouds, Cathán made his way to the covered ditch where Abhartach lay asleep. The ground was peaty and covered with thick moss, so the approach of the big man was as silent as the grave. He drew his iron sword and when he saw the mound of earth move he lifted his weapon high, and struck the mound with the full force of his body behind the blow. A horrific scream echoed over the hillside, and at that moment the moon emerged from behind the clouds.

Blood was seeping through the moss, and when Cathán pulled it away the face of Abhartach was exposed. It was a grotesque sight, with a mouth twisted in the most evil grimace that Cathán had ever seen. So bad was it that Cathán covered the face with his own cloak so that he wouldn't have to look at it. He wrapped his belt around the body and with a heave that was no more than a featherweight to a man of Cathán's stature, he flung the body over his shoulder and carried it to a rocky place to bury it.

Cathán went back to his own place, content in the knowledge that Abhartach would never terrorise the countryside again, or so he thought. But sure, he'd forgotten the belief of the ancients that if a person is buried in the upright position, facing his enemies, then he will have even more power over them than he had when he was alive. Sure, those druids of ancient Ireland knew a thing or two for what do you think happened next?

I said that Abhartach was a magician as well, didn't I? Well, didn't the vanquished dwarf rise again the very next day and this time he brought a harp with him and lured the unwary with sweet music. As soon as he had them in his grasp he was back to his old carry-on of demanding a bowl of blood from the veins of his victims to feed his evil corpse. What could Cathán do but come back to hunt him down?

Now, Abhartach had learnt a few lessons from his first death. He was not going to be so easily found. He went across the hills and searched until he found a cave. The entrance was so small that only a man the size of himself could slide in. He gathered a few rocks and pulled them across the small opening and contentedly fell asleep.

By night he waited for any living creature that dared to be abroad. It made no difference to him if his victim was man or beast, although he declared to himself that there was nothing sweeter than a young maiden, and these he wooed with his music. His appetite for blood became insatiable as the nights wore on and he began to be a bit careless. This was what Cathán was hoping for. The people of the area no longer went out at night; they locked up their animals in their barns and their families in their houses, for they certainly weren't going to take any chances.

Cathán needed to draw Abhartach out if he was to kill him, so he conversed with his trusty Irish wolfhound and asked him if he would be willing to act as bait. His dog trusted him implicitly and Cathán whispered the instructions to him. He still had the cloak that he had wrapped around the dwarf the first time, so the dog got the scent and set off at a rare pace. Cathán, for all his large size, was fleet of foot, and within a short time the wolfhound came panting back to his master.

One of the things you should know about Cathán is that he had a great understanding and empathy with animals. There was not an animal that he couldn't converse with, so when his hound told him where Abhartach was, he wasted no time. Again he approached quietly, wanting to catch Abhartach unawares, but he saw that the entrance to the cave was too small. He determined that he would wait for the monster to come out. His eyelids began to droop and, although he valiantly tried to stay awake, he began to dream of the lovely woman whom he hoped to make his wife. He settled into a beautiful dream and contentedly snored, forgetting all about his mission. But where would a man be without his dog?

Just before the first rays of sun crept over the hill the wolfhound's ears pricked up and he let out a low growl deep in his throat, loud enough to wake his master. Cathán realised then that Abhartach was not in the cave, but had been out on the hunt for more blood. He sent the hound into the cave and hid himself behind a gorse bush. Abhartach made terrible guttural noises as he approached, and it was clear that he had not had a successful night's hunting. He hunkered into the cave and the last thing he expected was that he would be grabbed about the throat by sharper teeth than his own. The dwarf managed to slide out of the cave while still trying to hold back the hound intent on ripping his throat apart. As his

hand reached to his knife sheath, Cathán cleaved him at the back
of the neck and killed him. Like before, he wrapped him in his
cloak and carried him to a windswept part of the mountain to
bury him a second time. But this time he piled more rocks high on
top of the grave.

Would you believe it, but the bold Abhartach rose again and
escaped from the grave, throwing the rocks to one side? No one to
this day knows how he managed it, but manage it he did. He set
about a more bizarre reign of terror, changing from one form
to another, and those he caught he used them more cruelly and
viciously than before, for the killings and burials had inflated his
temper and his appetite for blood was loathsome.

Cathán, tired of the whole thing, decided that he would take
some advice as to how he could kill Abhartach and bury him in
such a way that he wouldn't rise again. He went to a druid and
asked his advice on how to vanquish this tyrant. The druid took
the cloak that Abhartach had been wrapped in and swung it
around seven times before he spoke, 'The one you seek to kill is
not really alive, he is one of the *neamh-mairbh*, or walking dead,
and the only way he can be safely restrained is this; leave aside your
sword of iron and fashion one of yew wood. Drive it into the heart
of this monster. Then you must bury him upside down. This will
teach his followers a lesson, for I have read the signs and there
are many walking dead waiting for him to rise. Let Abhartach
be buried upside down, for this is the rite that will deprive him
of a restful afterlife. Fill his grave with rocks and clay, place a
boulder atop and encircle it with a ring of thorns. In this way he
will be imprisoned by the fairy folk, for should the stone be lifted
Abhartach will arise.'

Cathán thanked the druid and on the way home cut a thick
branch from a yew tree. All the next day he whittled it into a sword
and tested it on a rock. It was surprisingly strong. Cathán was ready,
and decided to tackle the monster head-on, armed with the sword.

His wolfhound led him to the new abode, a rocky inlet on Lough
Neagh where Abhartach had made his home. He swam through the
waters and spoke to the eels there. They understood what they were

asked to do. They slithered into the inlet and wound themselves tightly around Abhartach neck and tightened their living noose until he was nearly dead. Cathán raised the yew sword high, then plunged it with all his might into the heart of Abhartach. He carried his lifeless body to the place now known as Slaghtaverty and buried him upside down with his head closer to hell, as the druid had said. He searched and found a huge stone and placed it over the grave-stones and encircled the grave with hawthorns.

That was the third time Abhartach was killed, and he rose no more, for hadn't Cathán asked the fairies to watch over it? And it is said that the reason the ground is raw and clear of plant life is that the Giant's Grave is cursed ground.

Never again did Abhartach terrorise the people of Slaghtaverty.

N.B. The land on which the Giant's Grave lies has a reputation of being 'bad ground'.

Some years ago, when workmen were clearing the site, they had several unexplained accidents involving a chainsaw. They were attempting to cut down the tree, but the saw stopped dead without explanation, but when it was removed from the site it started working again.

There were attempts made to lift the heavy boulder but again, a strong iron chain snapped, hurting one of the workers, and when his blood spilled on the ground the earth seemed to heave and give a sigh.

Were these just pure accidents or was Abhartach attempting to show that his magic powers had still survived into the twentieth century?

12

THE MAN WHO
RAISED THE DEVIL

Poteen had a terrible hold on some people in rural parts and there were plenty of people to distil it in the hidden caves and gullies in the Sperrin Mountains of County Derry. It was often brought out on a '*ceilidhe* night' when the neighbours gathered together. Sure, when the dancing and eating were over more poteen was poured and the stories became wilder and wilder.

One man, after drinking a bit of poteen, declared that he knew the right words that could raise the devil, but his pronouncement was greeted with great hilarity. The man lost his temper, pulled himself up to his great height of five-foot nothing and shouted out the words. To the awful fright of all the people in the room, the Devil materialised in their midst.

They rushed to the door, but in their haste only one man managed to get out before the door and windows slammed shut. Try as they might, they could not open them. They screamed to the man who had spoken the words to make the devil disappear but, unfortunately, he either didn't know the words or couldn't bring them to his mind when it was so utterly drink-befuddled.

Well, the Devil flung himself around the room, throwing the dog and cat to the wall and smashing everything in sight. The terrified people gathered underneath a crucifix on the wall and began to say the Rosary, which enraged the Devil even more.

Fortunately, the man who had escaped through the door had run for the priest, who came armed with holy water and a crucifix. He sprinkled the blessed water on the door and it opened. When he entered the house he held out a large crucifix before him. He could hear the shouts of the people huddled in the other room and called out. 'May the Lord spread his mantle of peace over you and rid you of Lucifer.'

There was a spine-chilling screech from the upper room where the people were gathered and the house trembled with the sounds. He bade the man behind him to come close.

'Follow me and spread water to the four corners of the room, but don't let it go near the fire or the chimney.'

The man held the bottle of holy water and did as he was asked. The two entered the upper room, and at the incantation of the priest the shape began to change grotesquely. The body disappeared, leaving only a strange tail, and the face swelled into a monstrous mask that resembled some unknown wild animal, with gaping jaws and fiery-red eyes.

The priest approached it, holding the cross before him and praying. The man with him sprinkled the water, and with each drop the manifestation shrank in size. It backed away towards the fire and, with a terrible scream, it disappeared up the chimney.

The priest's hair turned white and his face became so wrinkled that the people in the upper room did not recognise him except by his voice.

Apparently that man who called up the Devil never spoke again till the end of his days when he prepared to meet his God. And wasn't it strange that poteen-making ceased in that townland?

13

DAN AND THE DEVIL

An old man in his late seventies, by the name of Dan McCluskey, came into Derry to have a suit made. When he came into the shop my grandfather, who was a tailor, was sent to measure him.

'This,' Dan said, 'is going to be my last suit, for it'll be the one that I'll be laid out in when I go to meet my Maker.' So he warned my grandfather to do a good job.

'The neighbours and the mourners will judge me by the cut of it and I wouldn't like my Maker to turn me away for want of a good bit of tailoring!'

While the measuring-up and pinning was going on, my grandfather and he chatted, and so outrageous was the story that Dan told him that my grandfather was afraid to repeat it for fear of being thought foolish. But then one night, when he had a couple of pints of stout in him, he let it slip, and from then on he recounted it if he was asked.

It started when Dan was a young man and was travelling all over the Derry and Tyrone, working on farms. 'Where there were farmworkers to be hired I was the first to knock at the farmer's door and ask for a job and begod, when they heard who I was, for the cut of a body goes ahead of a body where labouring is concerned, they took me on right away.'

On one farm in County Derry the farmer told him to fill the cart with manure from the midden (the place where the dung from the byre was thrown), and to bring it out to the other farmworker, who would scale it over the potato field.

'D'ye know that each time I wheeled out that cart full of dung that fellow was sitting on his backside, smoking his clay pipe. At the beginning, I was near ready to grab that pipe and break it over his head but sure, the dung I'd brought out before was already spread. I can tell you now that it puzzled me, for as long as it took me to fill the cart with the smelly stuff he had it spread rightly in less time. No matter how quickly I filled and carted the dung I still couldn't keep up with Andy, for that was the name of the man in the field.'

At this stage of the telling, my grandfather always paused and had to be goaded into getting on with the tale.

'Well,' he would continue, 'I always asked how that could be done and was Dan not working hard enough? And sure he nearly ate the face off me for suggesting he was a slow worker.'

'Deed and I was not,' said Dan, 'didn't I tell you that my working ways went ahead of me in the country? I was one of the best and never wanted for a job.'

Another puff of the pipe from my grandfather and then he resumed the story.

'Begod,' said Dan, 'I never worked as hard in my life and that fellow hardly had a sweat up, even though what would have taken the best part of two days was done in a half day. I didn't mind having it done, but I was getting paid by the day, not by the amount of the work done, like Andy, and I said so.' At this, Dan was a bit het-up, as my grandfather always related.

'Aye,' said Andy, 'I take your point, so I'll tell ye what we'll do. When the midden is half cleared we'll sit down and have a smoke because you're right. It wouldn't do us any good to let your man know that it was done and done fast.'

Now, Dan was an honest Ulsterman and he'd never sat down on a job before, but Andy persuaded him to rest for a while anyway. He offered Dan a smoke and made room for him to sit on the barrow.

'How did you manage to spread that stuff as fast as I could get it to you?' he asked Andy.

'Why would ye do that dirty work?' Andy answered, 'Sure haven't I a friend who can do it quicker and better than the both of us?'

'Who?' said Dan to him, 'I'm looking around but narry a person do I see.'

'Well,' said Andy, 'he doesn't like to be seen unless you call him up, if you know what I mean.'

Dan was still puzzled, but Andy had a strange smile on his face and it sort of concerned Dan, so after the smoke he rose and began to lift the manure with the pitchfork, but the other man stopped him.

'Didn't I tell you I had a friend? Put down that pitchfork or my friend will be thinking I don't trust him.'

When Andy began to fill his pipe again and stretch himself out at his ease Dan felt more uneasy.

'Look,' said Dan, 'I might want to come back here and work again and the farmer needs to know that I'll do the work, so I better get on with it.'

'I lifted that pitchfork and when I turned to lift the dung,' Dan recounted, 'didn't it begin to spread itself all over, up and down the potato rills. Begod! It fair took the heart from me. I never saw such strange goings-on in my life. And all the while that fellow Andy just kept smiling.'

'See?' he said, 'I told you. I have a friend.'

'Where the hell is he then?' said Dan, 'because as far as I can see there's nobody here but you and me, and as soon as I get me coat on there'll be nobody here but you!' And he ran.

When Dan came by that way again at harvest time the farmer told him to go out and help in the field. The same man was sitting at his ease, smoking just like before, and his job this time was to cut the crop with the scythe, and Dan was to rake it up and put it into stooks. But Andy did no such thing and somehow the work was done.

'I put up a few stooks myself, but every time I looked around another one was up beside it.'

My grandfather questioned him, but the man was adamant that the stories were true, because he saw it all himself. Maybe my grandfather was nervous or whatever, but he accidently stuck a pin in his finger and it bled.

'Begod,' said Dan, 'There's another thing. We cut ourselves on the barbed wire, and I bled like a pig and there wasn't a drop of blood came out of his hand. Makes you think, doesn't it? The neighbours said that that man was in league with the Devil.'

My grandfather didn't believe in the supernatural but he said that hearing that story made him shiver and he was glad when Dan left.

14

THE DEVIL AND THE BISHOP

There is a story in Foster's Ulster Folklore about a Ballymena bishop who cheated the Devil, but sure, the same story is said to have happened to the Earl of Bristol, Bishop Hervey of Derry and Raphoe Diocese. The incident took place in Downhill.

Now, if you've a mind to understand what happened, it would be wise to peek behind the titles of bishop and earl to the man, Frederick Augustus. He was a fine man, most people agreed, admired for his grand wit and culture, and wasn't he known for his love of the arts? But he wasn't what you might call a conservative man of God. Indeed, he was known to have a great liking for the women and he was certainly not monogamous!

In fact, many a story got about concerning what you might call his munificent nature, all of which suited his grandiose ideas of himself. Sure, didn't he like to wear stylish clothes that were more expensive than any that the gentry or lords could afford? If they were eccentric, sure, that just seemed to echo his peculiar behaviour. This is the sort of thing he was known to do to get people's back up; as part of a dare he once proclaimed himself to be agnostic, and King George III referred to him as 'that wicked prelate'.

Would you believe that some of Hervey's clergy reported his behaviour to the King, saying that they suffered sadistic treatment at his hands? But then, isn't it the way of ambitious men, even those in the 'holy' Church, to try to take down those in authority?

Especially when they see themselves being more suited to the position than the one who is in it.

One of the complaints these ambitious clergy had against Bishop Hervey was the way he attacked them about their over-indulgent figures. Sure as God, I'm not telling a word of a lie, he ordered them 'to address their portliness' before he would promote them. You can be sure they hated the bishop when he ordered them to run through bogs and marshland at night that they might shed weight and be worthy of higher Church positions. The bishop's reasons for choosing night time may have been to save these men embarrassment, but they didn't choose to see it that way. It was said that their barely concealed hatred multiplied when he sat in his coach, checking that they were doing what he asked. Looking at his portraits today we can see that the bishop himself was no stripling, so what the clerics weighed is open to serious deduction.

It's likely that it was his attitude towards these poor, indulgent men of the cloth that prompted the Devil to visit Bishop Hervey in his library where he relaxed on one of his irregular sojourns to his diocese.

This wasn't any ordinary library. It was really a bit of an extravagant folly called Mussenden Temple, built in 1785 and dedicated to the memory of Hervey's cousin Frideswide Mussenden. Not content with just an ordinary building, he risked getting on the wrong side of his fellow bishops by asking the Pope's permission to copy the style of the lovely Temple of Vesta in Tivoli, near Rome. Wouldn't you know that he had seen it on one of his numerous visits to Italy and thought that it might brighten up the rocky headland at Downhill?

Can we just imagine that he was sitting there reading, with a blazing fire in the hearth and the rain beating a tattoo on the windows that overlooked Benone Strand when whoosh … in came the Devil, manifesting himself in front of the bishop. Now, Bishop Hervey, who was fond of a joke, had at some stage tricked the Devil into believing that he would bargain with his immortal soul, and the time had come for the Devil to offer something in return; for it's common sense that the soul of a bishop must be worth more than that of an ordinary man. The bishop, however, was quite sure that a man of God could outwit the Devil and that was his reason for tempting fate.

That evening the Devil found him reading his Bible by the light of a candle, and the bishop asked him in a very mild voice if he could wait until the candle, which was well burnt down by this stage, would finally go out.

The Devil agreed and waited, and he moved closer just as the candle flame was dying. But the good bishop slammed the Bible shut on the Devil, rendering him helpless. Wasn't he the clever one?

You can be sure that that Bible was never opened again, and before the bishop went traipsing around Europe he took great care to lock the Bible away. Now, wouldn't you know that such a gallivanting type would die abroad just to create another wee bit of drama?

It was in the year 1803, at the grand age of seventy-two, that the bishop took his last breath in Albano in Italy, and his body was returned for burial to Ickworth parish church. At his written request the locked Bible was buried with him.

So we will never know if the story of the Devil locked up in the Bishop's bible is true or not. I would bet that good is victorious over evil any day.

15

THE DEVIL AND
THE GAMBLERS

Howard Street is one of those very steep streets that begin on the high ground just outside the city walls at Bishop Gate. When Derry was an island bounded by the Foyle and a small river, this gate would have been its highest point. Outside of the gate was good land and there was a thriving farm in the earlier years after the plantation of the city. A man named Milligan had owned it, and although he was long gone to his rest it was still known as Milligan's Farm. Probably it had once been quite large, but gradually it became smaller, until only the farmhouse and a few outbuildings remained.

When the farm was burned down in the early 1900s one of the buildings was saved and a blacksmith bought it for his forge. It was a handy place for farmers and traders to come and have their horses shod when they were visiting the fairs and their business had gone very well. Shoeing horses and making cartwheels was the owner's daytime occupation, but he had a bit of love for gambling, so after dark he ran a 'card school', and it was a popular pastime for many of the local men who enjoyed the gambling after an hour or two of drinking. It must be said that the amounts were small because they were all family men and money was hard to come by.

Derry men are a friendly lot, so when a stranger came into the pub one night they made room for him at the bar counter, and gradually the conversation turned to the card playing. The man seemed interested, although he professed that he wasn't very good at the gambling. But after a few drinks they were feeling expansive and invited him to join them at the forge.

The stranger was true to his earlier statement, for initially he lost some money, but since he didn't seem too perturbed by it and was obviously enjoying himself the men began to bet a little more money. Still the stranger lost, and they all left the forge that night with heavier pockets. During the next few nights, the stranger was on a definite losing streak and began to bet a little wildly. The men matched the higher amounts, knowing he would lose, but then gradually, there was a change and he began to win.

Thinking it was just luck, the men continued to match the larger amounts of money as the stakes went higher and higher. The men were definitely betting beyond their means and the stranger kept winning each time. One man bet all of his wages and, in desperation, he made the remark that he would sell his soul to beat the new man. At that the stranger thumped the table and laughed, and the cards scattered everywhere. There was a scramble to pick them up and it was only when they reached under the table that they saw the cloven feet of the stranger. Shocked and frightened, they realised then that they had been entertaining the Devil in their midst.

You never saw such a scarpering for the door as they did that night. The stranger held the arm of the man who had made the remark in a tight grip, and he screamed for the others to come back. Between them they managed to pull him free and then ran hell-for-leather down Howard Street into St Columb's Wells, the street of the Holy Well of Columba. By the time they reached it they were panting with fright and exhaustion.

'What'll we do?' they cried to each other, fearful that the Devil was following them.

One of the men started pumping the water and when the man whose arm the Devil had caught pulled up his sleeve they turned ashen at the sight of a bright red imprint of the Devil's fingers. When the man saw that, he screamed aloud and drenched his arm with the water, all the time reciting a prayer. A terrible stench came from the wound, but as they watched the imprint disappeared and the man's skin was as smooth as a baby's bottom.

He blessed himself and declared, 'That was another miracle of St Columba.'

At that very moment they saw flames light up the night sky and an unearthly scream rent the air. They went home that night, chastened men, and were unaware that the forge had burnt to the ground until the following morning, when they passed and saw that it was only a smouldering heap.

Now, that's the story as I heard it and, like all stories, there might be a bit of exaggeration, but it's well remembered that none of those men ever gambled again.

16

THE WATERSIDE GHOST

*I have to thank Sean McMahon for the translation of this story from
the Irish language. Sean is a well-known writer, raconteur, actor and
a very generous person. I have used some artistic licence in the telling
(as most storytellers do), so please do not compare it to the original!*

There was a young fellow called O'Doherty, who lived with his
two aunts and an uncle in the Waterside. They took him in and
cared for him after his parents died as he had no other relatives.
They were right glad that another young fellow, named Meehan,
moved in next door as he would be company for their nephew.
In no time at all they became best friends, and this lasted right
through childhood. They did the usual things boys do, getting into
scrapes together and looking out for each other. Being the same
age, they went through school together, from primary school right
to the time that they both decided to go to Maynooth University
to study for the priesthood.

While they were there, the O'Doherty boy's uncle died and when
he went home he found his aunts in a state of shock and distress
because of the suddenness of the death. He offered to stay at home,
but it was important to them that he continue with his studies,
so back to Maynooth he went. There were no prouder people than
they when he was ordained on the same day as his friend Meehan.
But, as was the way with newly ordained priests then, there were too

many priests to service Ireland so they went off to other countries like America, England and Scotland and it was no different for these young men, for their paths took different directions. Fr O'Doherty was sent to serve in Glasgow and Fr Meehan was appointed to Moville parish, along Lough Foyle.

Now, it seems that strange things began to happen in the house where the two aunts lived. From eleven o'clock each night a 'dead light' was seen to shine, and was accompanied by strange animal noises. As it grew near to one o'clock in the morning the mysterious noises grew in volume and the light became more brilliant, so much so that the old aunts couldn't stand it and went to stay with friends, declaring that an evil spirit was haunting their house.

Well, there was great curiosity in all the neighbours and even a bit of fear when they gathered to see what this manifestation was. As you can imagine, word soon reached Fr O'Doherty in Scotland, but he wasn't able to leave his parish just then to go home to see what was wrong. So he got in touch with his dear friend Fr Meehan and asked him to go to Derry to find out what was amiss.

Fr Meehan didn't quite believe the stories that his friend had heard, but he set off for Derry to see for himself what was happening, and when he arrived didn't he find a great crowd there huddling around the house, waiting for the 'show' to start. Within a couple of minutes, right on the dot of eleven, the unusual light was clear to be seen, and when he heard the terrible grunts and groans of some strange animal with his own ears he hastily sent to the Long Tower church for a priest to come and assist him. Very soon afterwards an old priest arrived in a horse-drawn sidecar. He stepped out of it and told the driver to stay where he was. Sure, the crowd parted when they saw the priest, for they knew that this man could do something about the haunted house.

When he reached Fr Meehan he asked, 'What do you think of all this?'

Now, the priest was indicating the crowd with his hand but Fr Meehan thought that he was just talking about the house, and answered that he knew very little other than that which the parish priest could see and hear himself.

'It's a bit of a circus here, but we'll proceed. Have you ever done an exorcism before?' he asked.

Fr Meehan felt the fear creeping up his back and shook his head.

'Well, you're going to help in one now, young man. I want to light a candle before we go in there, but tell me, is there any place in the house that the spirit could be driven to and secured?' asked the old priest.

One of the neighbours overheard and volunteered that there was a storehouse behind the house built out of brick, with an iron half-door, but that it hadn't been used for years.

'Go and unlock it then,' ordered the priest, 'and bring me the key, for we'll not proceed till that's done.'

Once that door was unlocked, Fr Meehan lit the candle and the parish priest led the way to the stairs. When they reached the bottom stair the candle abruptly went out. Fr Meehan relit it and the same thing happened – the candle spluttered out! At that, the old priest became very angry and he rushed out to the street, grabbed the whip from the driver of his sidecar and came back into the house with it.

'I'll go in first and you follow behind with that candle and keep it lit!' he commanded.

Fr Meehan felt the sweat break out on his body and confessed later that he would rather have stayed outside but, egged on by the parish priest, he followed behind him to the top of the stairs. At that stage he was weak with fear and then, in the corner of the room, he saw a figure. It was tall and there was a malevolent stare in its eyes, and when it came out into the light of the landing window the evil thing appeared to be a goat that could stand and walk on its hind legs.

The Long Tower priest pointed a finger at it and, trembling with rage, he yelled, 'Come out, I demand that you come out!'

The goat began to move forward, and the parish priest motioned to Fr Meehan to stand back, whispering, 'I'll go ahead and when it follows me, you make sure to stay behind it. Take this,' he handed Fr Meehan a phial of holy water, 'and sprinkle it behind him so that it can't go back.'

The priest ordered the 'thing' to follow him but it held back, making guttural sounds in its throat as the ominous light moved frantically across the wall.

'I order you to follow me, in the name of the Lord.' The goat made a screeching noise, the same noise that the neighbours had heard each night only this time it was so loud that the house almost shook and Fr Meehan put his hand to his ears.

'Stop that!' shouted the parish priest to him. 'Hold the candle high and keep your nerve. I've seen this before. I need you to do what I say.'

Fr Meehan jumped back as the figure sped past him, leaving such a stink in the air that he was almost sick. The priest made the sign of the cross, and when the figure cowered in front of him, Fr Meehan sprinkled the first drops of the holy water. Step by step, the priest led the goat down the stairs and out the back to the storehouse. The door was open and the priest ordered the 'thing' inside.

It obeyed.

The priest locked and bolted the door, and that was that.

When they went outside the old priest scattered the crowd with a few well-chosen words; 'There'll be no more disturbances, so go home to your beds and say your prayers.'

He got into the sidecar and went off, leaving Fr Meehan staring after him. He felt drained yet euphoric at the same time. He needed to do something, so he went to see the two aunts and they were right glad to see him.

'Will you be going back to the house now that it's been blessed?' he asked.

'Ah no, sure, we're very happy here and what use would it be going back? The landlord can rent it out once we have our bits and pieces out of it.'

Now, new tenants moved into the house and they were English. Of course they heard some rumours about why the house had lain empty for so long, but it was a good house and they fixed it up to their satisfaction but what happened?

In the year 1926, in the month of November, there was a night of thunderstorms and gales, and right after that the sounds and the light reappeared. The tenants were terrified and sent for Fr Meehan when the neighbours told them about the previous manifestation and how it had been banished. When Fr Meehan investigated, he realised that on the night of the high wind the storeroom roof had been blown off and that was how the evil thing must have been set free.

He wasn't about to tackle it on his own so this time he went to the bishop and told the story. Didn't the bishop come with him and they went through the same procedure as before? This time though, they led the evil thing into a deep coal cellar, the door was not only locked and bolted but cement was poured in and there was no way for the manifestation to escape.

No one knows why the 'thing' appeared and took up residence in that house, for the aunts and uncle were good-living people. But then, it is said that the Devil is always on the lookout for new victims.

17

CAHIR RUA O'DOHERTY

Sir Cahir O'Doherty's sword, a long, heavy, iron weapon, is usually on display in the Tower Museum in Derry. Now, if a small man tried to raise the sword, never mind lift it high enough to do some damage with it, he would be putting a stress on himself. Despite the size and weight of the weapon, Cahir Rua (Cahir of the Red Hair), used it to great advantage, slaying enemies here and there and everywhere in Ulster. Sure, that says more about the calibre of the man than any words of praise.

He was one of the remaining Donegal chieftains in the six-teenth century, over six feet tall, with red hair and broad shoulders. He was a fancy dresser too, and wore a Spanish hat with a tall plume, and he cut a dashing figure even though he had an arrogant way with him. The fact that his distinguished appearance made him an easy target in battle didn't seem to worry him.

By all accounts, he welcomed the chance to show his prowess with the sword and, like many other chieftains, he was a willing collaborator with the English Crown, especially in the Nine Years War (1594-1603) and afterwards. Sure, he had a great reputation as a fearless fighter. It's no wonder then that Sir Henry Dowcra, the English military commander and governor of Derry, was his patron. Sir Henry was clever enough to know that a man like Sir Cahir was better as a friend than a foe, and if anything hap-pened among the Irish around Derry, Inishowen or Tyrone, then

Sir Cahir was a great man to have on your side. Cahir Rua was knighted by Lord Mountjoy, but to his dishonour and shame as an Irishman, he served as foreman of the jury that pronounced the absent earls who had fled to the Continent in 1607 as traitors. Now, you might ask yourself how much more loyal to the Crown or disloyal to his Irish roots could a man be than that he would denounce his fellow earls? Sure, we'll put that to one side for the moment, since our story happened after 'The Flight of the Earls,' his fellow chieftains' exile.

When this firebrand loyalist turned rebel in 1608 it came, as you might well imagine, as an unbelievable shock to King James I, for this young, handsome man was known as 'The Queen's O'Doherty'. Just a few months before he led his rebellion he was currying favour and was engaged in trying to become a member of the Prince of Wales' household, such was his desire to be a person of note in the English court. What would ail an Irishman that he would want to do that?

Now James I and his government were probably wondering why this leading member of the Irish aristocracy was trying to ingratiate himself into the royal household, and then how could he so suddenly turn his back on that honourable prospect to lead a dramatic revolt in Derry in April 1608. Poor James I was hard put to understand where he had gone wrong in his judgement, and probably asked himself would Cahir have defected if he, James, had agreed earlier to having the Irishman as a member of his household? I'm sure that question must have caused him sleepless nights, especially when he began to hear of Sir Cahir's exploits against the Crown.

But in O'Doherty's eyes he had very good reasons for it. Some Crown officials in Derry were jealous of this young man who seemed to have the King's favour, never mind valuable and sizable estates. However, being an Irish Catholic in those days, never mind a Catholic with land, his status was far more precarious than he realised. He felt safe as long as Dowcra was governor but he wasn't to know how soon that situation was to change, for, in 1606 Sir Henry Dowcra sold his position as governor of Derry to Sir George Paulett. Unfortunately, this man was known to have an awful greedy way with him and had no respect for Irish people in general or Catholics in particular. From the outset, he had his eye on Sir Cahir's vast estates in Derry and Inishowen.

Isn't it strange that someone else had the same idea? For at about the same time George Montgomery (of the same family as the much later Second World War field-marshal) the first Protestant Bishop of Derry, Raphoe and Clogher, arrived in Derry, and he was no less jealous or greedy than Paulett. Isn't it shameful when men of the Church have ambition like that? This bishop set out to get his hands on O'Doherty's lands too, but wasn't he a crafty one, for didn't he turn to English law? And in the courts in Dublin he sued Sir Cahir for land in Inishowen. When the bishop won his case, Sir Cahir lost faith in the British justice system and was ready to turn his back on England.

Well, he held off for a while until a more personal insult came his way. That came about when Sir George Paulett, playing the big man and attempting to show his disdain for the Irish, and his hatred for Sir Cahir in particular, punched Cahir in front of his own men. That was definitely waving a red rag at a bull. O'Doherty could not be seen to lie down under such an insult and took his revenge by seizing the fort of Culmore, a few miles from Derry, on the shores of Lough Foyle.

The next night, 19 April 1608, he attacked, sacked and burned Derry where Paulett, to Sir Cahir's eternal delight, was killed in the fray, whether by Sir Cahir himself or by one of his men is not known. But the private view of the English Privy Council was that if Paulett hadn't lost his life in the rebellion, he would certainly have been executed for having provoked it.

Once Sir Cahir O'Doherty started the attack he found it hard to stop, and his enemies should have known that he had a temper to match his red hair. He didn't stop at burning Derry to the ground. No, he rampaged through the country and Strabane was burned soon afterwards. Wouldn't you know that the revolt wouldn't stop there? It began to spread across the province as factions of the other clans joined the rebellion. Poor auld Cahir was on the run from the English and when he was killed at the Rock of Doon near

Kilmacrennan the revolt died, and Sir Arthur Chichester's men crushed the remaining dissidents. Chichester came out of it well because he received the entire lands of Inishowen for himself as a reward. Sir Richard Wingfield recovered Derry in 5 July 1608, but received little for his trouble.

At the end of the day, although the English Privy Council acknowledged that there were perhaps justifiable reasons for O'Doherty's revolt, but he should not have rebelled against the crown.

Their anger was reflected in a contemporary Protestant pamphlet which spoke in very bitter terms about the native Irish, and how they would stab the English in the back. The pamphlet claimed the blood of the English was as music to the Irish at a banquet, that the serpent never conceals his enmity more shrewdly than when he conceals it in amity (or in friendship). It argued that, in response to O'Doherty's revolt, Ireland and the Irish like O'Doherty should be rejected. Instead of being assimilated into the burgeoning English system, Ireland was to be rejected 'as a bastard'.

Imagine a sentiment like this being circulated to the English public. Ultimately, it certainly influenced the Ulster Plantation in 1610, for didn't England take away much more land from the Ulster Irish than might otherwise have been the case? They planted their own people on it, although we've heard that they had to bribe some of the guilds to move over to Ulster.

The story of Sir Cahir's death needs telling, for he detested the fact that many Scots had requisitioned the rich lands along the Foyle and Swilly estuaries (even before the plantation of Ulster), and it was his not very worthy reaction that eventually led to his death.

Sir Cahir's aim was to expel these Scottish intruders that he saw as a scourge on the native people. One of these Scots was Sandy Ramsay, and in his absence, O'Doherty burnt down his home and slaughtered his wife and children. Sir Cahir may have been proud of his conduct on the battlefield, but many felt that this act against an innocent family put him on a par with the hated Chichester, who was known to indiscriminately slaughter Irish men, women and children. Sir Cahir doing the same thing suggested that he was lacking in nobility, and much as the Irish liked to fight, they didn't like to see women or children used in any war as revenge.

It was no wonder that the Scot swore vengeance and, aware that there was a price of five hundred marks on the head of the chieftain, he lay in wait at the Hill of Doon, knowing that Sir Cahir and his entourage would eventually come back to that place. They came yearly on Holy Thursday, for the Rock of Doon is famous as being the place where the Abbots of Kilmacrenan inaugurated the chieftains of Tyrconnell.

While a man waits he builds up an awful anger, and Ramsay was no different. He reflected on the great wrong done to him and his family, and by the time O'Doherty appeared Ramsay was crazy with renewed grief and seeking the worst possible revenge.

He knew the chieftain's swagger, and was well acquainted with tales of his pride (especially his flaunting of the hat with a heron's plume) and he soon he espied him, strutting around in his arrogant way.

Because it was Holy Thursday, Sir Cahir expected that a friar from the Abbey of Kilmacrenan would come to celebrate Mass at the rock on that day. The chieftain relaxed, chatting with his men, and Ramsay took his chance. He levelled his matchlock rifle, took aim, and a ball smashed through Sir Cahir's head.

With the gun's report echoing around the valley, the men thought that the English were attacking them and they ran off, leaving their fallen chieftain prostrate on the ground. Ramsay, being canny, waited to make sure that they were all gone, and only then did he slither down the hill to his victim. With every slice of his knife severing Sir Cahir's head from his body, the Scotsman thought of his wife and children. He wrapped the head in his plaid and set off to Dublin to claim his reward. (After all, he was Scottish.)

At nightfall, he stopped at a cottage owned by Terence O'Gallagher and sought a night's lodging. It was well known to Ramsay that Irishmen will never refuse shelter, and after a simple meal he lay down with Sir Cahir's wrapped head below the bed.

But Irishmen are not simple. Terence rose in the early hours of the morning and saw the Scotsman's gruesome plaid where the blood had seeped through. Very gently, without waking Ramsay, he lifted the plaid and recognised the red hair and features of the O'Doherty, for they were well known to every man in Derry and Tyrconnell.

He also knew of the hefty price set on this head. It would be enough to give him a comfortable life away from the barren lands of the north if he could bring the head to the English in Dublin. Happy with his find, he went off, leaving the Scotsman snoring.

Ramsay was like a man demented when he woke up and found his prize gone. He set off in pursuit, but when he asked people along the way if they'd seen O'Gallagher they sent him off in so many directions that he ended up back where he started, in Kilmacrenan.

So Ramsay, by his crazed questions and actions, spread the word far and wide of how he'd been duped, and the people laughed behind his back. Although there was great sadness at Sir Cahir's demise, there was great joy that no money-seeking Scot was going to gain by it.

In Otway's *Sketches in the North and South of Ireland* the story is still told with delight about how an Irishman, without treason, reaped the reward for Sir Cahir's death.

It is sad to relate though that the English displayed his head on a pike at Newgate as if he was a common felon, a fact that the Irish found hard to forgive.

18

ROBERT LUNDY AND THE GREAT SIEGE

Did Lundy really sell the keys of Derry for a bap?

St Columb's Cathedral is the oldest building in the city of Londonderry, built in 1633. It was the first post-Reformation cathedral in the British Isles. The foundation stone in the porch reads:

ANO DO   *CAR REGIS*
1633   *9*

If stones could speake
Then London's prayse
should sound who
built this church and
Cittie from the grounde

If they could speak, would they tell the true tale of Lundy, the traitor?

On 18 December every year a huge effigy of Robert Lundy, the erstwhile governor of Londonderry during the Great Siege of Derry 1688-1689, was suspended from Governor Walker's Pillar on the walls of Londonderry. It was set alight amidst great shouts of jubilation and drum rolls, and it was seen all over the west bank of the city. Of course, the famous city walls towered high over the Bogside and being the closest dwellings to the walls, the sight of this huge figure afire was more fearsome to those who lived below. Even though the IRA blew up the pillar, the tradition was not allowed to disappear. Nowadays, the effigy is suspended from scaffolding near the Courthouse in Bishop Street and set on fire.

'The Burning of Lundy' still gathers a great crowd, and a stranger happening on the event might ask, 'Who was Lundy?' Mostly he would get the short answer. 'He was the traitor who tried to sell out the loyal citizens of Londonderry.' The longer answer is as follows:

Lieutenant-Colonel Robert Lundy was dispatched northwards from Dublin to Derry by Viceroy Tyrconnell to pacify the Protestants, and Mountjoy's regiment was under his command. James II had promised Lundy that he would be governor of Derry, and that was a fine feather in his cap.

When Robert Lundy realised that the citizens of Derry were vehemently anti-James he swore allegiance to William and Mary on 21 March. He was re-commissioned as Governor of Derry by William and commanded the garrison in Derry under the Williamite banner. Meanwhile Richard Hamilton's Jacobite troops made their way to Strabane and on 15 April his troops routed Lundy's at the Battle of the Fords. Lundy's troops were 'driven from their trenches by the fire of Irish muskets' and had 'scarcely a dry short left in their pouches'. Lundy told his men that all was lost and the terrified shouts of 'To Derry! To Derry!' ended the battle.

Sure, it must have been an awesome sight when the cavalry thundered towards the pike men with their swords raised, slashing apart any man who stood in their way. It struck terror into the ranks of the Lundy's soldiers. Nobody could blame them for breaking ranks and fleeing back to safety behind the city walls, especially when Lundy led the retreat.

You see, in spite of that humiliation, Lundy remained a man with an attitude of superiority and that did not endear him to those under his command. Although he had underestimated the opposing forces at Strabane he continued his commission as if nothing had happened. He did not let the defeat deter him from his plans to strengthen the city's defenses. He had the walls and the gates repaired, he refitted gun carriages and musket stocks and removed buildings outside the walls, which might provide cover to besiegers. He increased the firepower by buying powder, matchlock rifles and cannonballs and had a protective bulwarks built that might be help to repel the Jacobite forces.

But all this work did not atone for the debacle at the Fords and at the Parliamentary Commission held that Lundy's lethargy and lack of leadership were lamentable and his conduct was viewed as detestable. Still, Lundy must have been sorely depressed, watching his great plans to save the city fall apart. He was a man who had earned honour and rank in foreign wars only to face defeat in a walled city, and a small city too, as it was then in the seventeenth century. It was no surprise that, having changed sides to save himself once, he would look for the best way to save himself if in danger again. Lundy's earlier loyalty to James counted for naught.

Another instance of what was later called Lundy's 'turncoat tendencies' and cowardice occurred on 14 April 1689, when English ships sailed up Lough Foyle to regain the city from its inhabitants. Lundy, on reading the king's letter presented by Colonel Cunningham, the commander, persuaded him that attacking Londonderry was hopeless, but that he would surrender the city if they only asked. At the same time he intimated to Cunningham that he intended to flee the city secretly.

When word of this leaked out and Lundy followed it by ordering that no fire should be returned when the enemy reached the walls, he lost his authority and he was accused of treachery and labelled a traitor. From then on his life was in danger.

Children in the city still believe that Lundy, starving and half-mad, sold the keys of the gates of Derry for a bap (a soft roll of bread). When we look at the quality and quantity of food available, the smell and taste of a fresh bap would be irresistible to some. For instance, the price of provisions, when they could be found were:

A quart of meal	1s 0d
One pound of horseflesh	1s 8d
One pound of tallow	4s 0d
One pound of salted hides	1s 0d
One pound of greaves	1s 0d
¼ of a dog (fattened by eating corpses)	5s 6d

A dog's head	2s 6d
A quart of horse blood	1s 0d
A horse's pudding (gut)	0s 6d
A cat	4s 6d
A rat, fed on human flesh	1s 0d
A mouse	0s 6d
A handful of sea wreck (seaweed)	0s 2d
A handful of chickweed	0s 1d

Did he live to fight another day? Where St Columb's Hall now stands there stood the Pear Tree Tavern, named after the tree that once grew there. Lundy was supposed to have shinned down that very tree to escape. It is said that he was helped by Revd George Walker and Captain Adam Murray. He was arrested in Scotland and sent to the Tower of London, but it remains shrouded in mystery how Lundy eventually did manage to escape from Londonderry.

To add fact to myth there is a chair made of the wood from that pear tree in St Columb's Cathedral. The tree was apparently blown down in the great storm of 1844.

Isn't it a fact also that those who were once held up as heroes and saviours within any culture and who fell from grace usually go down in history as villains. There is no better example of reviling a villain, perhaps anywhere in the world, than Londonderry's Lundy's Day, when the giant effigy of Lundy, wearing a placard

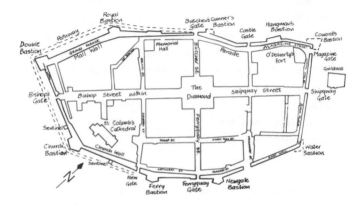

around his neck proclaiming that he is a traitor, is consumed by
fire within the revered walls of the city.

Just as Quisling, Captain Boycott and Charles Lynch's names
have gone into the English language, in Northern Ireland being
referred to as a 'Lundy' is synonymous with being a traitor, and that
is the ultimate insult.

But the success of the siege caused the city to gain a new nickname,
'The Maiden City', by virtue of the fact that its walls were never
breached during the siege.

A local newspaper, *The Sentinel*, stated that the importance of
the siege of Derry could never be underestimated, not only in Irish,
but also in European history. Yet, within momentous events, local
myth, like the tale of Lundy, always has a place.

19

THE BLIND HARPER, DENIS O'HEMPSEY

You can say one thing about the harper, Denis O'Hempsey, and that is that he never let being blind get in the way of playing the harp like an angel. Maybe the fact that his father and mother were well-off landowners, owning much land between Garvagh and Magilligan, gave him a start. Still, it must have been a terrible cross for them to bear when their son lost his eyesight as a result of smallpox at the age of three. They could see that he had a *grá* for the music because when he heard a harper called Turlough O'Carolan playing, weren't his wee feet tapping the floor?

Well, his mammy needed no second bidding, she had a harp made for him and sure, he started playing as soon as he was old enough to hold the great thing. He had nothing else to do all day but practise his music and O'Carolan's lovely compositions were a pleasure to learn. His teacher, Brigid O'Cahan, taught him until he became better than she was herself at the playing. When he needed a new teacher she suggested John C. Garragher, who was one of the best musicians in the north-west and a renowned teacher as well.

John C. travelled all over the country playing for the gentry and when Colonel George Vaughan invited him to Buncrana Castle to play for one of his fancy gatherings, he invited Denis along. Sure, Denis wasn't able to see the grandeur of the place but he heard the murmurings of English voices and nearly left there and then, for he was an Irishman through and through. John whispered that these men could afford to pay big money for good music and anyway, it would be great practise for when he became professional if he could only settle himself to play for the likes of Vaughan. Let it be said that he outshone even himself that night and sure, after that he was in great demand.

But wasn't he always looking to better himself? And, as Denis was wont to say, 'Connacht is the best part of the kingdom for music and harpers.' This belief brought him further south on his travels, and he studied under Loughlin Fanning, and finally under Patrick O'Connor of Connacht, one of the most celebrated harpists in the country. Being taught by O'Connor was a dream come true for Denis O'Hempsey.

Now, Denis didn't forget his own folk around Garvagh, and when he came back and played for them they certainly showed their appreciation. What did they do but buy him a beautiful new harp that had the most melodious sound ever? Sure, he stayed up till the wee small hours playing it, and if it hadn't been for the big shout he let out, they would have been lulled right to sleep.

'Glory be!' said Councillor Canning, who had presented the harp earlier, 'what ails ye?'

Denis held up his hand. 'Look,' he said, 'look.'

'What is it man?' said Canning, very perturbed, for he could see nothing.

'Can you not see it? I can feel it. I broke my nail.' Now, that was a bit of a disaster for Denis, for he was like the harpists of old who played with their fingernails and not their fingers. The gathering couldn't see what his annoyance was for until he demonstrated the difference on his harp, for with the nails he could play the most intricate pieces with great dexterity, except for the note that finger with the broken nail touched. They were full of the wonder that makes an Irishman just shake his head. Sure that's what happens when the words aren't there and that, you may agree, is an unusual thing in itself, for Irish people had the gift of the blarney without having to kiss the Blarney Stone.

When Denis listened to the silence he began to laugh, at himself as much as at them, and they spent the next few hours listening to his witty repartee, for wasn't he a great entertainer and full of the auld talk.?

That sort of amusing talk, as well as his musical ability, is probably what got him as far as Edinburgh to play for Bonnie Prince Charlie. Although, it is said, O'Hempsey could play 'The Coolin' and the 'Dawning of the Day' with such sweetness that you'd have tears in your eyes just listening.

You'd think with all his rambling around the two islands that he wouldn't have had time to marry, but he was no chicken when he did. He just turned 86 when a young woman from Magilligan married him. His music must have put a spell on her, for didn't she shock everybody and give birth to a daughter? Now, that was a stroke of good fortune, for that wee girl ended up looking after him in his 'declining' years. Sure, you would have thought that he was well declined by then, would you not? Wasn't he the lucky man!

In 1792 there was a big Harp Festival in Belfast, held to save the old traditional airs from disappearing, and it's no wonder that he was the oldest of the ten harpers there. The harp that was given to him so long before was still the only one he played.

He spent more and more time in his cottage playing his beloved harp, often playing it far into the night. But so sweet was his music that carriages would draw up and, unbeknownst to him, the occupants would stay quietly outside, listening to him play.

Even on his deathbed he plucked out his favourite tune, 'Eileen Aroon', and then he sank back onto his pillows with a smile on his face. He was 112 years old and when his death was announced.

'The last of our bards now sleeps in the ground,' said the report.

The blind harpist's instrument was preserved in Downhill. The front and sides are of white sallow and the back is fashioned from bog fir, patched with copper and iron plates. It is silent now, but the following lines are engraved upon it:

> In the days of Noah I was grown,
> After the flood I've not been seen
> Until seventeen hundred and two I was found,
> By Cormac Kelly underground.
> He raised me to that degree,
> Queen of Music they call me.

THE RAPPAREE, SHANE CROSSAGH O'MULLAN

Shane Crossagh O'Mullan had a plethora of names. He was called a highwayman, a rapparee and an outlaw, amongst other things. But whatever you called him, he was a likeable fellow by the sound of things. It's the truth that the Derry people saw him as the 'Robin Hood' of the downtrodden people of the county.

Sure, it's a well-known fact that when the Plantation of Ulster took place the land was taken away from Irish tenants to make way for English merchants from the different guilds of London. If your house and land happened to be on the land that they were granted then you were evicted. Often skulduggery was used to strip the tenants of their land, as was the case with Mr O'Mullan.

Shane's father had a wee plot of land in Tullanee in Faughanvale, but when the land was parcelled out to the Grocer's Guild he was only there on sufferance, and the bailiff was on the lookout for any excuse to put him off the farm. It seems that he reported that his son had been insulted and Shane's father was evicted. Now, that was a terrible injustice for a man to lose his livelihood, and him with a young family to feed. What could he do but go from field to field with his one cow that he was 'allowed' to keep and rely on the help of his neighbours?

When you're a young man and see your family treated like that the anger is fierce, and although Shane was resentful of the wrong done to the family he still did his best to help his father. One evening at dusk, he sneaked back to cut grass on the old homestead in Tullanee to feed to the cow. He was caught and managed to get away, but to escape further punishment the family retreat to the mountains above Claudy to a place called Lingwood.

Now, Shane wasn't on his own in feeling hard-done-by. Oh no. There were many other young fellows like himself whose families were thrown off the land and they banded together with Shane as their leader. It's no lie that some of them were bent on vengeance and even on plunder, so you can add the name 'desperado' to the list, for desperate they were to get their own back on the landlords.

Sure, Shane had a way with words and was quick to talk himself out of a predicament. One day he was out walking when he saw some pheasants and his mouth watered, for he could almost taste and smell the roasting of them. He stuck his pike in behind some gorse bushes and went back to his house to get his gun, but on the way two young men rushed at him and, before he could catch his breath, they had him secured with his hands tied behind his back.

'Bad enough,' said Shane to them, 'as I had appointed to meet a friend, and I find it hard to leave my bottle of poteen that I had intended to treat him with.'

The two men looked at each other, 'Let us have the poteen then, and we won't put you in irons.' Shane put on his downcast face and agreed, and they went with him to the hiding place where the bold Shane pulled out the pike, disarmed his captors and sent them on their way.

When he arrived at the house, his father was not alone. Dominic, the schoolmaster, Roddy the soldier and Parra Fada (Tall Paddy) were with him.

'Where were you,' asked his father, 'and us waiting here for you.'

'In the Devil's Claws,' said Shane, 'and I got free by thrashing soundly two strong lads and taking these pistols from them.'

Said the schoolmaster, 'What a pity the avenues of promotion are closed to you, for if things were otherwise than the fighting and feuds around us, you'd be a credit to your country.'

'Master, you've a hard tongue,' answered Shane, in Irish.

'Indeed Shane, I'd advise you to go to the magistrate and get his pardon, for if you resist again they'll brand you an outlaw and then what will become of you?'

'If I were you,' said Roddy, giving the schoolmaster a dirty look, 'I'd take to the hills and live off the wealthy budachs.'

'In other words, be a robber!' said Dominic, 'For the love of God, man. What are you thinking of?'

Shane's temper rose. ''Tis no robbery to take back some of the ill-gotten gains of the wealthy. The landlords robbed the people of their money and their lands by the authority of the king.'

Dominic answered, 'Then you're making a robber of that king, for what right had he to give what was not his own? It is my advice that we should submit to what we cannot mend.'

'I will walk the ladder to the top of the gallows,' said Shane, 'before I submit to tyranny.'

Shane's father tried to talk some sense into him and get him to cool his temper, but his son would have none of it.

'Sure, and I'll take to the hills with you,' said Parra Fada.

Roddy approved, saying, 'If I had a regiment like the two of them, sure even the strongest fort would fall.'

Dominic was shocked and hurried from the house, leaving the three to plot and plan and therein lies the beginning of the Rapparee's reputation of taking from the rich to give to the poor (from the Irish *ropairí*, meaning half-pike or pike-wielding person).

One of Shane's earliest robberies took place at twilight in the district of Maghera. He met a landlord who had purchased land from one of the planters who had, in turn, been granted the land by the king. Shane waved his pistol at the man, and the victim acted in a distressed state, but pretending that he was not a pistol-carrying man himself.

'Stand and deliver up what you rob the people of,' demanded Shane.

'I am no robber,' he answered Shane.

'I thought you were a lawyer who lived by robbing the public.' Shane poked the pistol in the man's side.

'I am a landlord,' replied the gentleman, pulling himself up to his full height, which wasn't very high.

'Oh, then, you must have big estates and you're the very robber I want. 'Tis well-known that you take the sweat of the poor man and rob him of the fruits of his industry.'

'My good man, do you mean the tenants who pay me for my land?' said the gentleman.

'Your land!' said Shane, 'Pray, who gave you that land?'

'My father.'

'Who gave it to him?' By this time Shane's temper was getting a wee bit overheated, so he prodded his pistol deeper into the man's side.

'My father purchased it from the owner and the king gave it to that owner.'

'Aye,' said Shane, 'the king who stole it from the good people of this country. Enough of this! Hand over your purse.'

As soon as he got the money, all of twenty pounds, Shane turned away, and he heard the landlord click his pistol. At the sound he bounded over the hedge shouting, 'You prepare for the battle after you are beaten and by then it is too late!'

The people of Maghera would be telling you more than I am, suffice it to say that there were several other stories about Shane robbing the rich to help the poor around there.

Now, that very same night he came across a family whose only cow was impounded for tithe. The man went by the name of McKenna and he was evicted by an agent and thrown out to live on the roads with his wife and four children. Shane, thinking of his own family being evicted, went after the agent and, in a rage, pulled him off his horse and robbed him of ten pounds, four of which he gave to McKenna. That was the sort of man he was.

But he wasn't always robbing for so called altruistic reasons. One morning he got up and realised that his clothes had a bit of a smell, verging on a stench, so he robbed a rector of thirty pounds to buy himself a new suit of clothes.

He was swanking around in his new clothes and was caught off-guard, arrested and brought before a magistrate who confronted him with the three others he had robbed in the area.

'What sort of a man are you,' said the judge, 'to be robbing people of their livelihood?'

The magistrate wasn't too impressed when Shane spat on the floor of his nice courtroom, so much so that he ordered that he was to be lodged in Derry Jail. As good timing would have it, there was a crowd of soldiers on their way from Belfast to Derry and they put Shane under guard.

Well, wasn't Shane the crafty one, who knew the Carntogher Mountains like the back of his hand? When they stopped for a rest Shane boasted that he would show them three leaps that would astonish them.

'But,' said he, 'I need my arms to balance, so could you take off these manacles for a minute?'

Sure, as soon as he was free of the irons he leapt to his feet and bounded down the mountainside with the soldiers in full pursuit. They tried to follow him, but he hid out in Dungiven. The soldiers were getting all sorts of reports about his whereabouts and the next day they heard that he was in the woods near Ballykelly. The wily Shane saw them coming and when they were close to him at Slaughmanus he made for the river, hoping to escape them. He ploughed through the fields, sinking into the wet muck, and when he reached the river sure, wasn't it greatly swollen after the heavy rain? He made his way as far as the Ness (a waterfall), and, undaunted, he leaped over it at the precipice. It is said that a farmer, seeing him jump the river called out, 'Bravo Shane, 'tis a great jump.'

'It ought to be,' was Shane's reply, 'I had a good race for it.'

Ever since, that spot at the river has been known as Shane's Leap. Some people even say that his ghost has been seen making the leap again and again because it was necessary to prove to those who doubted that he did it even the once.

Even when you're on the run as an outlaw you have to eat, and Shane and his comrades caught a nice fat rabbit in the Ness Wood, which is about six miles from Derry. They decided that for once they would like a hot meal, for they were fed up of eating cold rabbit food. Shane called in at the house of Mr Hasson to ask if he could cook it. Sure, the servant was up to her eyes cooking bacon for the harvesters and there was no room on the fire for Shane to use. Well, didn't the servant get very annoyed when Shane didn't leave? And there was a bit of an altercation, during which the pan of bacon was upset. Didn't the flames shoot up as soon as the hot fat hit them and the thatched roof went on fire? The harvesters in the field saw the flames and rushed in, seized Shane and tied him to a cart and set forth for Derry Jail. As the cart went along Shane freed his arms from the rope and at The Oaks Lodge he whistled. His comrades, recognising the call to arms, rushed out of the woods, overpowered the guards and unbound him. Shane was free to fight another day.

But sure, Shane's exploits continued, and the one that he's most famous for happened nearly by accident. Shane and Parra Fada were staying for the night in a tavern kept by a man called Fowler, about midway between Dungiven and Carntogher. They were in a private room, and from it they could hear the conversation of the travellers without being observed. They often stayed there and the landlord gave them the nod when a likely traveller came in. Isn't that how they knew who to rob?

On that particular night there was a detachment of cavalry, led by General Napier, staying at the inn. When Napier was sitting at the table eating his dinner, didn't he hear about some of the exploits of Shane and his men? He was, to put it mildly, disgusted that men such as these could be allowed to roam the countryside, robbing the virtuous of their money. Well, didn't the bold Napier boast how he would deal with an outlaw such as Shane Crossagh O'Mullan? He was heard to say, 'The best way to quiet a country is a good thrashing, followed by great kindness afterwards. Even the wildest chaps are thus tamed.'

Shane, being a man of instant temper, as we know, was fit to face down the General there and then, but Parra Fada held him back. While the General ate and drank his fill, they plotted how Shane would get his revenge. They left ahead of the cavalry and selected a long narrow bridge on a road passing through a bog, near Feeney. He arranged the turf in high banks along the road on both sides and placed hats on top of these and on the bridge to give the impression that armed men sheltered behind them.

Darkness had settled in by the time the detachment of cavalry reached the bridge. Shane aimed and shot Napier's horse from under him, and the alarmed troopers gathered around the general to defend him.

'Surrender!' shouted Shane, 'I am Shane Crossagh!' His voice echoed over the glen and sent terror into the hearts of the cavalry.

'Ready boys,' he roared to his imaginary followers behind the turf stacks, and at the same time he threatened instant death to the first soldier who would raise his arms in defiance. He ordered Napier to hand over his sword and then demanded that the soldiers lay down their arms and submit to be tied with ropes, two by two.

By that time the other rapparees arrived, having been alerted by Parra Fada. They seized all the arms and money, and Shane stripped the now angry but impotent general of his uniform. Shane put on the general's uniform and insisted that Napier put on Shane's modest outfit. He refused to put on Shane's old caubeen (beret), appealing to the outlaw's manly character. Shane strutted around in the general's uniform and retorted,

'You had not that high opinion of me at the inn, when you called me a cowboy, so on the caubeen must go. It's the man that makes the general, not the clothes!'

Didn't that general rue his words? For Shane mounted on a charger and guarded the cavalry for twelve miles and marched them, now in their underclothes, towards Derry. When he arrived within view of it he left them with the injunction not to release each other until they reached the military headquarters at the Diamond.

But sure, didn't he stand trial at the Assizes in Derry for the offence, and him still dressed in General Napier's uniform? With his eloquent way with words, even in the English tongue, he pleaded his own case, showing that although all were at his mercy no one was even injured. Maybe he had some admirers on the jury, for not only did they acquit him but also, didn't they express their admiration for his bravery and his perfect control of his comrades? Isn't that something – a brigand on charges being admired by his jury?

After that Shane installed himself as a ranger. It was really as sort of protection racket that he had going, where the farmers would pay him tenpence every quarter to protect them and sure, wasn't everybody happy?

Except one man, a public robber, who refused to spare those under Shane's protection, and the two of them agreed to settle the dispute in an open fight. Sure, Shane wasn't going to let a man like that get the better of him, and after a couple of hours the robber fell down, stone dead, and that was the only murder that was ever laid at Shane's door.

But do you think the law was happy with 'freebooters' like Shane? Sure, doesn't jealousy and greed get in the way of a man trying to earn an 'honest' living? Didn't a magistrate, Mr Hunter, arrange for a weaver to entrap Shane?

Said the magistrate, 'When that man comes for his tenpence, do not rise to pay it. Let him take it.'

Shane called at his normal time and asked for the money. Now, usually the weaver kept it in a drawer, but that day he called to Shane that he was too busy right then and why didn't Shane go over to the drawer and take the money out and put it in his pocket? The weaver went to Mr Hunter and told him that Shane had taken the money and that was exactly what the wily magistrate wanted to hear.

He sent for Shane and treated him with great friendliness.

'Mr O'Mullan, would you do me a great favour?' said he. 'I have a letter that needs conveying to the governor of Derry Jail and I hear that you are the man who could deliver it safely. Isn't that so?'

'Indeed sir, I can do that,' said Shane, not for one minute thinking that the magistrate was anything but an honest man. So, off he goes with the letter and the request to wait for an answer for the magistrate. When the governor read the letter he put Shane in a cell and the tale that went down in history was that Hunter was a man of double treachery, asking Shane to deliver a letter that would put him in jail, for the letter charged him with forcibly taking the weaver's money.

When he was arraigned on the charge, the weaver was asked if it was through fear or through friendship that he allowed Shane to take his money. The weaver, fearing the wrath of the magistrate himself, swore it was through fear. Wasn't Shane found guilty and sentenced to the gallows?

Around that time the rapparees, having lost their leader, were in a bit of disarray and were not as careful as they might have been if Shane had been there. They too were brought to Derry and Shane nearly lost his mind when he heard that his two sons were among them, and that the judge passed the sentence that all were to be hanged with him.

What happened next shows the loyalty and the bravery of Shane. Colonel Cary of Dungiven Castle, who had connived in some of Shane's escapades, had the privilege of obtaining a pardon for one criminal each year and offered freedom to Shane.

'I will not accept unless my sons are pardoned with me.' But the Colonel couldn't do that, although he tried, and when he went back to give the news to Shane and to implore him to accept the pardon, Shane answered with stoicism, 'I am an old man now and cannot be long after them, so, with God's blessing, I will die with them.'

'Tis a sad end to the tale of the well-loved rapparee, for he died on the scaffold hanging between his two sons, in 1772, outside Derry Jail.

He was buried in Banagher Old Church graveyard overlooking the wild Sperrin Mountains, the scene of so many of his exploits and his beloved homeland.

The people of the area say that sometimes they hear Shane's call-to-arms accompanied by the sound of galloping phantom horses.

21

AMELIA EARHART'S FIRST SOLO TRANS-ATLANTIC FLIGHT

On 21 May 1936, a strange sound was heard over the city of Derry. The clouds were fairly thick but scattered and the sunshine managed to shine through in parts, but at first the cause of the drone wasn't seen. People in the Pennyburn area of the city came out of their houses and watched, shading their eyes as they looked up.

It was no wonder they were shocked, for as they watched they saw a small plane descend beneath the cloud cover. Rarely did they ever see a plane in the sky, never mind over Derry. As they watched it sink ever lower in the sky some made the sign of the cross, others stood with their hands over their mouths in amazement that quickly turned to consternation as the plane dipped out of sight over Ballyarrnett. When it vanished they waited to hear the boom of a crash but there was only silence. They looked at each other, and, not waiting to put on a coat or scarf, there was a mad rush up the Racecourse Road to see what had happened.

At the same time James McGeady and Dan McCallion were standing in McGeady's field in Ballyarnett when they heard the drone, and they couldn't believe their eyes when they saw the plane clip the top of the trees bordering the next field. They too waited for the sound of a crash landing but the only sound was the putt putting of an engine, then silence as the engine went dead.

They ran across the field. Neither gorse bushes nor fences deterred them. Only when they spied the plane did they stop and look at each other, not sure if their eyes were playing tricks. The two men had never set eyes on a plane so close up before. Wondering what on earth it was doing landing in Gallagher's field, they began to run towards it, leaping over the last fence.

As they approached, the cockpit cover slid open and the pilot stepped out. It was only when she took off her helmet and brushed her fingers through her thick, short hair that they realised it was a woman. By the time she descended quite a breathless crowd had gathered to see this unusual sight. There was great excitement as people pushed closer to have a look.

James McGeady, trying to look nonchalant, lit up a cigarette and stood beside the cockpit, whereupon Amelia Earhart, for that's who the pilot was, turned to him and asked him to extinguish it quickly because there was a leak in the petrol tank.

'Where am I?' she asked, looking around.

'You're in Gallagher's field,' was the answer.

For some reason there was a photographer from the *Daily Sketch* on hand, and he had the scoop of the season, catching the moment after Amelia landed the plane. A young boy, Patrick Lynch, and the lady pilot were photographed looking straight at the camera and sure, that boy fed on that story till he was man big, and why wouldn't he?

As Amelia walked with the men to Hugh McLaughlin's house nearby they plied her with questions which she answered with good humour. She must have been exhausted, considering that she had just completed a transatlantic flight, never mind it being the first solo flight by a woman across that wide ocean. She had set off the day before from Harbour Grace, Newfoundland and hadn't had a wink of sleep since then.

After some food and answering questions for a few hours, Mr Gallagher invited her to stay in his house in Springtown. She was glad of the offer for, although people didn't really know about jet-lag then, that's not to say she didn't suffer from it. Although the mayor offered her deluxe accommodation in the best hotel in Derry she refused, preferring to stay in the Gallagher's home in Springtown for a few days. She was feted in the city wherever she made an appearance. Boys-o-Boys, never were there so many photographs taken, and the news spread all around the world and brought glory on Derry.

Hundreds of telegrams, tributes, and accolades poured in for this brave woman who had completed a journey that many men believed a woman could not do. After that 1932 solo flight, women in the United States and throughout the world claimed Amelia Earhart's triumph as one for womanhood. At a White House ceremony honouring her flight, she said, 'I shall be happy if my small exploit has drawn attention to the fact that women are flying too.'

Amelia was a Kansas girl, born in Atchinson in 1896. As a teenager she worked as a military nurse in Canada and became fascinated by the stories of the early aviators. While she was doing social work in Boston she heard of a Trimotor plane being prepared to fly from Newfoundland to Britain. She applied for and was accepted as a passenger in 1926 on the plane *Friendship*, and in so doing Amelia became the first woman ever to make a transatlantic flight.

She met and married George Putnam, and he was happy that she wanted to go on with her flying career, even accepting that she wanted to retain her maiden name. His support didn't stop at that, for he financed many of her flights across the United States after her solo flight to Ireland. It was just as well that he was a man with money, because flying in those days was an expensive and dangerous occupation.

Derry people kept a close eye on her exploits through the newspapers and indeed, felt proprietorial about her. When she flew the first solo flight across the Pacific to Hawaii they were just as excited as the Hawaiian people she met on the islands in 1935. She was a great girl for setting the records for solo flights.

But her bravery and ambition was to be the death of her. In 1937 she set off with her navigator, Fred Noonan, to attempt the first around-the-world flight in a twin-engine Lockheed Electra. After completing two-thirds of their circumnavigation they set off for

Howland Island in the Pacific, and that was the last anyone ever heard of them or the plane. Earhart's sense of adventure knew no bounds and people hoped that the pair would reappear, having magically survived, but that was not to be.

Like all disappearances, myths have grown up around the vanished plane and its occupants, but no one knows for sure what happened. In that sense it fits in with the cult of Irish folklore, where we weave our own imaginings around the facts with the idea that a good story is worth embellishing with a few twists and turns.

Amelia Earhart's emergency landing in Gallagher's field has already earned its place in Derry folklore.

22

THE LEGEND OF DANNY BOY

Oh Danny Boy, the pipes, the pipes are calling
From glen to glen and down the mountainside
The summer's gone and all the roses falling
'Tis you 'tis you must go and I must bide.

These are the opening words of the famous song that is sung all over the world wherever there's an Irish diaspora. Written in the English language, it is one of the most hauntingly beautiful songs of all time and Irish people abroad are often reduced to tears when they hear it. Even when people don't know the words they hum it and many ask,

'What is the story behind it?'

In the seventeenth century it was known as the 'Londonderry Air', but the tune is much older than that. Still, how did the name Londonderry come into it at all?

In the year 1608, King James I was trying to bring the wild Irish race under control, for they had given the English plenty of bother until their chieftains had fled the country in September 1607. The saying is true that 'All their wars are merry and all their songs are sad'. Sure, there's no sadder song than Danny Boy, is there?

Now, King James I gave Derry to the City of London Corporation and in 1613 the name was changed from Derry to Londonderry. Although there were strong political connotations to the name, the prudish Victorians thought that Derry sounded too much like the French word '*derrière*'. This word when translated and added to 'London' seemed quite rude so they spoke of it as the 'Air from County Derry'.

The words of the Londonderry Air are seldom sung, but it is the melody that catches the heartstrings, and it is to that melody that the words of Danny Boy were later added. But the melody was handed down, and among those suggested as its creator was Rory Dall (Blind) O'Cahan, a descendant of the ruling O'Cahan clan. Rory Dall lived sometime between 1560 and 1660, and when the O'Cahan lands were confiscated Rory was filled with anger and sadness. He was moved to compose the sorrowful melody called 'O'Cahan's Lament'.

There are some tales around Rory's writing of it, one being that he was drunk one night, when on his way home he stopped to rest, and it was then that he heard the fairies playing the enticing melody. He kept it in his head as he staggered home and once there he played it on his harp until he was sufficiently sure of it. Of course, being Rory, he added some embellishment here and there. Once he was sufficiently sober and confident that he could play back the music, he serenaded guests with it and that was the beginning of the legend of Danny Boy.

Now Denis O'Hempsey was another blind harper whose life spanned three centuries. He was born at the end of the seventeenth century, lived through the eighteenth and died at the beginning of the nineteenth, and was apparently related to Blind Rory. If we believe the story, he inherited much of Rory's repertoire.

The history of Danny Boy seems to be littered with blind musicians, for as we jump forward to the nineteenth century, Jimmy McCurry, a blind musician who lived between 1830 and 1910, frequently played his violin at the Limavady Market in County Derry. Jane Ross, who lived opposite the Burns and Laird Offices in the town, heard Jimmy play the beautiful melody and she was enthralled. She crossed the street and invited the fiddler to play the tune again for her so that she could annotate it. She passed the music on to Dr George Petrie from Dublin, who had spent his life collecting the ancient airs of Ireland. When Dr Petrie published

The Ancient Music of Ireland he included the melody and it was listed under 'Anonymous Airs' and referred to as a song.

The tune did not achieve fame until 1913, three years after Jimmy McCurry's death, and since he was blind, he would never have seen Petrie's book, which was a limited edition. It is a strange thing but Jane Ross never once named Jimmy McCurry as the source of the melody, and it was thought by some later experts, namely Malachy McCourt (who wrote a book on Danny Boy) and Michael Robinson, that Jane Ross, a middle-class lady who aspired to be one of the nineteenth-century British upper class, had no interest in a lowly fiddler apart from learning the melody and, 'may not have even entertained the concept that common folk had names, or that street fiddlers were not interchangeable'.

Jane's brother William, a collector of Irish tunes, had a different story to tell. He said that it was he who first heard the tune and whistled it for Jane and told her that he had heard it as he was passing a mountain cabin. Jane apparently went to the cabin, which was quite a way from Limavady, and the old man who lived there told her that his father had heard the tune played by a harper when he was just a boy.

The stories go on and on, but the fact that Frederic Edward Weatherley (1848-1929) was the author of the lyrics is not disputed. This started with the emigration from Ireland during the Great Famine. When the potato crop failed and the Irish people looked for a life in the New World they brought their music and traditions with them. There was a gold rush in Colorado and a relative of Fred's called Margaret heard the nostalgic tune played by one of the Irish miners and immediately sent it to Fred in Somerset in England. He had already penned many songs including 'The Holy City' and 'Roses of Picardy', and saw that lyrics he had already written would be perfect with the melody. He 'married the two of them to make one of the best-loved songs in history'.

In the year 1913 an Australian composer, Percy Grainger, recorded the song. On the sleeve of the record was the following note: 'Irish Tune from County Derry, harmonised in memory of Irish childhood friends in Australia.'

Because Fred Weatherly, in his autobiography *Piano and Gown* (1926), wrote of his hope that 'Danny Boy' would bring together the Unionists and Nationalists of Ireland, it is of little surprise that the song held so much appeal for the Irish people – and later, for people all over the world.

Yet the question was still asked, 'Who was Danny Boy, and why is there a song about him?'

Some say Danny was going to war and the song was sung from the pain and love of a young maiden. Others that his mother was singing to him, bidding him farewell as he set sail for the New World. She knew that she would never see Danny again, for America was so far away that emigrants never returned. Others say that a young woman was bidding farewell to an Irish chieftain, for it is a song sung by a broken-hearted lover. The reason is not important because 'Danny Boy' is about more than entertainment.

The moving and beautiful melody has made the song into a cultural symbol, a song of comfort and an anthem of the human spirit. Maybe Elvis Presley was right, and angels wrote the music after all.

'Danny Boy' is a legend – a Derry legend.

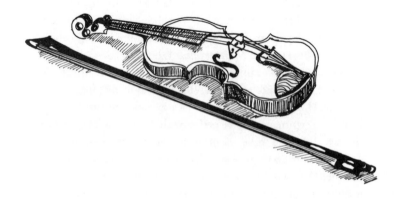

23

THE 116-YEAR-OLD WOMAN

Francois Thurot was a French privateer captain, who entered Belfast Lough and anchored off Carrickfergus on 21 February 1760, where he landed a body of 1,000 soldiers and sailors. He overpowered the garrison, took the castle, but didn't destroy the town. He called upon the people of the north to rally behind him to fight the English but they refused, mostly out of fear, it is said. This was an attempt by the French to distract the British forces during the Seven Years' War. So he set sail again, but his fleet was attacked at the Isle of Man. Although he was killed and buried at sea he won a hero's name for himself in France.

Even England lamented his death, for he fought for honour rather than plunder, and his successful landing at Carrickfergus was remembered with great satisfaction by the oppressed Irish Catholics and commemorated in lines commencing: 'Blest be the day that Thurot came here.'

Events like that can appear as dry words in the pages of a book, but one woman remembered Thurot's landing when she was forty years old. She was Margaret Magrath from Moneygran, near Kilrea. What is remarkable about Margaret is that she was 116 years old in 1836 and remembered not just the incursion but also the fact that he had three ships and held the castle for five days. Imagine having a first-hand account seventy-six years later.

In the Ordnance Survey Memoirs of Kilrea parish her appearance was described in detail. At that great age she lay in a foetal position, and she had some difficulty speaking in her old age. Alas there are no family details, which isn't surprising since she undoubtedly out-lived them all.

24

THE GEM OF THE ROE AND THE BANSHEE GRÁINNE RUA

The most famous banshee story is set in County Derry, near the town of Limavady (*Léim na Mhadaidh* in Irish, meaning 'the leap of the dog'). There is a legend that an Irish wolfhound followed the command of his famous O'Cahan chieftain to get help when the enemy was attacking the clan. To do so it made a terrifying leap across a gorge on the River Roe. On this crag, overhanging the River Roe, Dermot O'Cahan built his castle, and thus the name of the town came into being.

Dermot O'Cahan, an Irish prince of great standing among the sixty other Irish chieftains, ruled an extensive domain in the north. The Atlantic Ocean formed the northern boundary of O'Cahan's country (*Tir-Cahan*). Lough Foyle was its western boundary, and the eastern one was the River Bann. The Sperrin Mountains provided the southern boundary, and the craggy mountain of Benevenagh was in the centre of their territory. This is where the banshee, Gráinne Rua, believed to be the guardian of the O'Cahan Clan, dwelt in the other world. The O'Cahans built the Abbey of Dooneven (Dungiven), and its graveyard was the final resting place for their dead. It was unheard of for an O'Cahan to be buried elsewhere, and therein is the tale of Finvola, known as the Gem of the Roe, and Gráinne Rua, the banshee of the O'Cahans.

It was the custom for the young men of the clans to travel to different parts of the island of Ireland and to Caledonia, to act as foster sons to other chieftains. During their stay they learned the customs of other clans and, it must be said, as a result of these visits there were many marriages arranged between the clans. It must also be remembered that it was easier to travel to Caledonia (Scotland) by sea than it would be to travel further south in Ireland by land to visit Irish clans. So building relationships through marriage was a means of maintaining peace between the two countries.

Dermot O'Cahan, the chieftain, decided to travel to the Courts of Caledonia with his eldest son. Finvola begged to go with them and Dermot, finding it difficult to refuse his beloved daughter anything, agreed. As they neared the Western Isles a tremendous storm arose and buffeted them hither and thither during the night. Before dawn, the mast of their ship cracked, causing damage to the starboard side. The chieftain was certain that they would founder on the rocks, but prayed that they would be spared till daylight when they might be able to repair the damage. If not, then they would have to abandon ship and each man would have to fend for himself.

The storm abated with the coming of the morning light, and they saw that the ship was irreparable while they were at sea. Dermot commanded his son to stay with Finvola if he, himself, should not make it to shore. Just then they saw a boat rounding a headland handled by a young Highlander, Angus Óg MacDonnell, who, with remarkable courage and speed, managed to bring the O'Cahan's boat into safe harbour.

His father, the MacDonnell, Lord of the Isles, stood on the shore, a magnificent figure in full military garb, and his voice boomed out.

'Welcome to Islay, my friends. I bid you welcome to the island of Islay.' Angus carried the lovely young Finvola to shore first, and while the others disembarked he had some words with his father.

'I offer you the hospitality of the House of MacDonnell and the skills of my boat builders. Come, you must be hungry and tired.'

Dermot was reluctant to be under such an obligation, but he had no choice. 'I thank you for your offer, my Lord. I will stay for the time that it takes to make my boat seaworthy.'

The two chieftains found that they had much in common, and Lord MacDonnell showed great interest in the family of the O'Cahan. Young Angus Óg, meanwhile, spent much time in Finvola's company and fell deeply in love with her. When the time came for the O'Cahans' departure he boldly asked for Finvola's hand in marriage. Dermot refused, saying that his daughter was too young. He was dismissive and anxious to return to Ireland to see how the twelve castles that he had ordered built for his twelve sons were progressing, and had no wish to extend his visit to accommodate a marriage.

Not to be put off, Angus later visited the O'Cahans' land and met Dermot and his men hunting and feasting on the fertile lands at the foot of Benevenagh. He ordered two of his men to accompany Angus to one of his son's castles, where he would meet with him when his hunt was finished. Angus, anxious to meet with Finvola, found the wait interminable. He hoped that his father's letter of proposal for Finvola would not be refused. He secretly sent a message to her to let her know of his mission and that he was near. Finvola was overjoyed and determined that her father would allow the marriage.

When Dermot sent for him to come to his castle Angus decided that he would do whatever it took to persuade Dermot that he was a worthy suitor. At the meeting he handed over his father's letter and again he asked for Finvola's hand.

Dermot waved him away, saying that the contents needed much meditation before he could reach a decision. He consulted his sons about Angus's father's proposal that he should provide a dowry of twenty-four of chieftain's sons to be married to the same number of MacDonnell daughters.

As he waited, the young man was tormented with the fear that Dermot might refuse, but when he came back to Angus he said, 'I will agree to the dowry that your father demands, but I have two further conditions.'

'Anything,' said Angus eagerly.

'I give my consent if you honour these conditions. The first one is that when I part with my daughter I have your word that when she dies her remains should be brought back and buried in the old

Abbey of Dooneven. No O'Cahan will rest in peace in a foreign land. The second is that her twelve handmaidens will accompany her to ease her loneliness in a strange land.'

Angus agreed to these conditions and he and Finvola spoke their vows before their family, friends and allies, solemnising their marriage in the Abbey of Dooneven. Soon the time came to depart, and the young couple were ready to set forth to begin their life together. Finvola, sad to be saying goodbye to her beloved father and brothers, stepped on board with her twelve maids and twenty-four chieftains' sons and set sail for Islay, leaving a broken-hearted father behind her.

Their marriage was a happy one, but the tale that unfolds is one of tragedy. Finvola died after a few short years and Angus, broken with grief, could not bear to part with Finvola's mortal remains. Instead, he built a crypt of the finest white marble and each day mourned her passing. He forbade his clan to relay the news of her death to the O'Cahans, yet, at the moment that Finvola took her last breath, the O'Cahans heard their banshee, Gráinne Rua, howl from the top of Benevenagh Mountain and wail through the hidden caverns of Benbraddagh. She cried without stopping, from dawn to dusk, and through the night the wails descended from the mountains and along the valley of the Roe. Dermot sent messengers all over the O'Cahan land to find out whose death was the cause of such lamentations, but they discovered all of the clan alive and well.

With great sorrow, the chieftain deduced that his beloved Finvola must have died. He hurriedly launched his boat at Magilligan, and with Finvola's brothers set sail for Islay. On the island Sir Angus watched the O'Cahans approach up the firth, and the doleful sound of Gráinne Rua was joined by a choir of Scottish banshees bewailing the breaking of a promise given for her return.

When islanders swarmed towards the mourners, intending to prevent them from taking Finvola's body, Turloughmore O'Cahan drew his sword and called out in a thunderous voice, 'Stand back you faithless islanders, who can pledge your vows today and break them tomorrow. Any who dare stop us shall bite the ground underneath my sword.'

When one Highlander daringly rushed forward and drew blood, Sir Angus, now Lord of the Isles, called out, 'Stop. No strife, my friends. Finvola was honourably given to me. She came in love with me and shall depart in the same. The fault was altogether mine and if I erred it was only through too much love.'

The O'Cahans entered the castle and found it cloaked in deep mourning. Angus begged pardon for not allowing Finvola's body to be returned to Dungiven. The chieftain, knowing the sorrow of Finvola's death himself, asked Angus to return with them. And so it was that two mournful men sailed across the sea and into the Foyle estuary. When they approached Magilligan, Gráinne Rua's keening ceased and the air was still once more. The O'Cahans knew that their beloved Finvola had come home.

She was laid to rest in Dooneven Abbey burial ground and a lament, composed by the O'Cahan bard, Toal O'Cathan, was played as Finvola was laid to rest.

There are several variations but this is believed to be the one played on that sad morning.

> In the lands of O'Cahan, where bleak mountains rise
> Where fine ridged tops now the dusky clouds fly.
> Deep sunk in a valley a wild flower doth grow,
> And her name was Finvola, the gem of the Roe.
> The gem of the Roe,
> And her name was Finvola, the gem of the Roe.
>
> To the Isle of Abundae appeared in my view
> A youth clad in tartan, 'twas strange as 'twas true
> With a star on his breast, unslung with his bow
> And he sighed for Finvola, the gem of the Roe.
> The gem of the Roe,
> And he sighed for Finvola, the gem of the Roe.
>
> To the grey shore of Alba his bride he did bear
> And shed were the fond years these lovers did share
> For thrice on a hillside the banshee cried low

'Twas the death of Finvola, the gem of the Roe.
The gem of the Roe,
'Twas the death of Finvola, the gem of the Roe.

No more up the streamlets the maiden do hie
For wan her cold cheeks now, bedimmed her blue eyes.
In silent affliction his sorrow doth show
Since gone is Finvola, the gem of the Roe.
The gem of the Roe,
Since gone is Finvola, the gem of the Roe.

THE LOVESICK LEANNAN SIDHE

But like a lovesick leannan sidhe
She hath my heart enthralled,
Nor life I own, nor liberty
For love is lord of all.

From 'My Lagan Love'

Every county in Ireland has its own tale of the *Leannan Sidhe*, the fairy lover, and County Derry is no different. The story is told of a young man trying to withstand the romantic wiles of a fairy woman.

Hugh was an adventurous young man and wanted to see the world so, despite the pleadings of his parents, he set off. Well, he'd been travelling for about three years when he got word that his father was very ill and he set sail for home. Unfortunately, his father died before he arrived and his mother was beside herself with grief. He knew that he would have to stay at home. She was a good mother and he just couldn't leave her, so he set about trying to keep the farm going. To be a good farmer you need to have a love of the land, but since he wasn't a man of the soil at heart the farm began to get a bit run down. Within a year of his father's death his mother fell deeper into a decline brought on by melancholia, for she never got over the death of her husband.

Hugh took to the drink, and soon the farm suffered; crops weren't sown, fences went unmended and the house wanted the lick of whitewash. Sure, it broke his mother's heart to see her big son falling to pieces, and when she was dying she begged him to catch hold of himself, to stop drinking and to find a wife.

Now, Hugh was a man of his word and he took his mother's dying words to heart. As her body was committed to the grave he made her a promise. He'd never touch another drop of drink, even when the other mourners were drinking after the funeral. When everyone departed to their own farms he walked around the place and took a good fresh look at it.

'Right enough,' he said to himself, 'it's a mess of the place. I'll put this to rights and maybe then I'll be able to find me a nice girl to marry.'

Now, like most places in Ulster, there are seven girls to every man, so you wouldn't have too much difficulty finding a nice girl. Hugh was a fine, big man and had a grand way with him, though he was unaware of his own good looks. Sure, wasn't he the finest looking man ever seen in County Derry? He had hair as black as the raven's wing, and eyes as blue as the sunlit sea. He was tall and broad of shoulder and under his tanned windblown skin the powerful muscles rippled, having been built up from hauling in the nets filled with fish from the oceans of the world. Even the dissipation of the past year hadn't softened him up too much. All he need were the right clothes because, as his mother had often said, 'Clothes maketh the man.'

He began to clear the fields again for the planting and discovered that once he put the sea out of his mind he liked the land work. Still, at the end of the day it was lonely coming back into the house that had forgotten the touch of a woman. After a particularly hard day clearing the far field of rocks and trying his hand at building a stonewall he resolved to do the final thing that his mother had asked of him, and that was to find himself a wife.

Knowing that there was a big fair on the Monday at the beginning of August he went into Portstewart to buy himself some decent clothes. Coming out of the tailor's shop he stopped as if struck by lightning, and indeed it was lightning of a kind, for didn't he spy the most beautiful girl he'd ever laid eyes upon.

Oh, her hair was like a fire glowing in the sun, her skin was white, and on her cheeks were freckles sprinkled like gold dust. Poor Hugh was besotted at first glance, and as he made his way over to her he wondered if this lovely creature had a husband already. When he reached her side he looked down and she, catching his glance, looked up. Sure, wasn't that the truth of the saying, 'It was love at first glance?'

Didn't they chat as if they'd known each other all their lives, and as the sun began to set in the sky and the market emptied, he asked if he could walk her home.

'You can,' said she, 'but only as far as the bridge, because my father will be waiting near there, and he warned me not to have any truck with strangers.'

Hugh would have walked to the ends of the earth with her, but as they neared the bridge she stopped. 'No further, Hugh, and thank you.'

Hugh stuttered out the words, 'Can I call on you, Kate?'

They arranged to meet, and as the summer dipped into autumn they were as deeply in love as any young couple could be. When she decked herself out in her best clothes and went out of an evening, her father suspected that there was a man in the offing. Now, an elderly man depending on a daughter to see to him in his old age gets a bit obstreperous and selfish when a young man is in the offing. He determined that he would put off any man courting Kate, but he didn't let on to his daughter what was in his mind.

'Will you marry me, Kate?' Hugh asked her one night, and her smile lit the heavens, for wasn't she as besotted with him as he was with her?

'Aye' she answered, 'but you'll have to square it with my Da. Come round tomorrow night and see him.'

As Hugh was walking over the mountain road on the way home that night, a wind whistled up out of nowhere and he knew right away that it was no ordinary wind. His mother had warned him about the *Leannan Sidhe*, a fairy woman of great beauty wanting to carry off handsome young men who were betrothed to another. It was said that once she got her eye on a man he was going to be tortured by her presence until she finally ensnared him. So Hugh pulled his cap down until it almost covered his eyes and kept his head down too, looking only at the road. Didn't he know that any man, looking into the fairy lover's eyes was doomed to follow her forever?

Well, that *Leannan Sidhe* came to his side and wrapped the wind around him like a blanket, and he had to battle against it to move an inch along the way. She pulled and she hauled, but he would not raise his eyes, and eventually she tired of the struggle and let go of him. When the sound of the wind disappeared he looked around and didn't he catch sight of her on the hill, and she was burying something under a gallan rock (a standing stone). He took note of the spot and hurried on home, determined that the next day he would see what she had buried.

The dawn broke and Hugh rose, pulled on his clothes and went to the hillside, knowing that the fairy lover would not come out in daylight. He pushed the rock aside, for it was powerful heavy and there, underneath it, was a bag made of the softest leather. He looked around, lifted the bag, and it was heavy. When he undid the string he couldn't believe his eyes for the bag was chock full of gold coins, bright as the leaves of the buttercups growing in his field. All sorts of thoughts were going through his mind, but the main one was not to tell anyone about his find. He would provide Kate with any treasure she asked for when she was his wife.

That night he dressed in the fine suit the tailor in Portstewart had made for him and went to ask Kate's father for her hand in marriage. He noted that this farm was as neat as a new pin, that the cows were well fed and content, and the outside of the house was newly whitewashed, unlike his own.

'Well,' he thought, 'with my gold I can fix up my farm and Kate will never want for anything.'

Kate was waiting for him at the door. 'Me Da's in a right 'aul mood and he'll try to make you lose your temper. Now I'm warning you, hold onto it, for it will do us no good for you to lose it.'

He nodded and she brought him in. Her father was sitting in front of the turf fire and he neither rose nor took Hugh under his notice at all. Hugh went forward with his hand out in greeting.

'Hello Mr Logan, I'm pleased to meet you. Here,' he said, 'Kate told me that you smoke the pipe, I brought you a couple.' He held out the clay pipes and Kate's father took them, looked at them then threw them on the hearth, where they smashed. Hugh stood with his mouth open and Kate's eyes beseeched him not to retaliate. He stepped back and squared his shoulders.

'I've come to ask for your daughter's hand in marriage, sir,' he said, his voice was strong with passion.

'What! If you think that I'd let my daughter marry a ne'er-do-well like you, you have another think coming. You, with not a halfpenny to your name, your run down farm and dirty house and no cattle. You, who drank like a fish of the sea that you sailed on and drove your poor mother into her grave. How dare you think that you would make a suitable husband for my Kate? Get out of my sight and don't come back!'

Before he could stop himself, and forgetting what Kate had said about not losing his temper, Hugh retorted.

'I've got plans sir, and gold aplenty, more than every man in this parish put together, and I can tell you that Kate would never want if she marries me!'

'You! Where would you get gold when you're scarcely scraping a living out of that dung heap of a place you call a farm?' By this time, Kate's father was on his feet and pointing to the door. 'Come back here when you can prove it. Until then, get out!'

Kate took Hugh's arm and he could see the sheen of tears in her eyes. Outside Hugh held her in his arms. 'I'll be back and I'll show him. Don't worry. We'll be married by Advent, I promise you.'

Hugh went on his way home, all the while debating in his mind about showing the gold to Kate's father, but sure, wasn't the love of his life worth it? He was so deep in thought that the cloying wind was on him before he had a minute to compose himself. But just in time he remembered, and when the *Leannan Sidhe* started her pulling and hauling again he was able to resist her. Aw, but he knew she was angry and that it wasn't the end of her trying out her wiles on him. He was fair exhausted by the time he arrived at his own wee house.

That night he stayed up and scrubbed the place from end to end. He blackened the pots and painted the crook over the fireplace and even whitewashed the side of the chimney. Once he started he couldn't stop, for if Kate's father agreed to let her marry him he was going to bring her back to the cottage the day after to have a look at her future home. In the morning he took every bowl, cup and plate from the dresser and painted the wood a lovely bright blue. He rummaged in the big cedar chest at the back of the room, where he knew his mother had stored her linens, and there he found the nicest curtains and tablecloth.

By the time he had finished he was ready to go to Kate's house, and he set off with the bag of gold in his pocket. The old man refused him entry and Hugh went to the wall outside the cottage door and spread the gold coins along it. With three steps that were almost jumps Mr Logan was at the wall, fingering the gold.

'I won't ask where you got it young man, but,' and at this point he slapped Hugh on the back, 'you can marry my daughter when the house is fixed up and the farm running well.'

Hugh blinked, 'that's too long a time.' He reached out and took Kate's hand. Her father stared greedily at the gold and thought.

'I'll tell you what, young fellow, I can have your farm fixed up in no time because I have strong workers. I can start you off with a herd too but I'd need to hold onto this gold for safekeeping. Would you trust your future father-in-law to do that, hmm?'

Hugh was so overjoyed that he and Kate could marry soon that he agreed, and true to his word her father did everything he said, although between you and me, he didn't have to spend but a fraction of the money. Every time Hugh enquired, Mr Logan had another wee job to do with the money, and the wedding was a grand excuse. When the couple married, the people came from miles around to celebrate the union, because country folk love nothing better than a wedding to get them all together. And what a wedding that was, with not a penny spared. If they wondered about the transformation in the farm they didn't pass any comments.

When the jollification was over the young couple snuggled down in their own bed, but before there was any funny business, a strange sound came to the window. It chilled the heart of the young man, for he knew that it was the accursed *Leannan Sidhe*.

'What's that, Hughie, darlin'?'

'It's only the wind, my love,' he said and he lulled her to sleep with his kisses. The same thing happened many times after, but always Hugh gave the excuse that his house was higher up the mountain than her father's and the wind was only to be expected.

All went well until Kate received word that her father was ill.

'Of course you'll have to go down to see him, and if you need me I'll come.'

'Who'd look after the farm, Hugh, if you go? Don't worry.'

He brought her to her father's and was relieved that he wasn't too sick.

'I'll be home by next week,' she promised him as she kissed him goodbye, and on his lonely walk home he began to hear the rustle of the wind, and it grew louder and louder and then he felt the grasping fingers of the fairy woman pulling at him and trying to carry him away, but he kept his eyes downturned, as always, and after a long time she left him with a fearful loud moaning of wind.

That night, although Hugh was exhausted by the tussle and pulling of the *Leannan Sidhe*, he took a long time to fall into a fitful sleep, tossing and turning restlessly in bed. The rattling of the wind on the window disturbed him, and still half-asleep he went to check that it was closed. When he opened the curtain without thinking there she was, staring at him with eyes as dark as the bog pools and her long hair glistening like the setting sun, and he was enthralled. With no more than a whisper he followed her to the Other World.

What seemed to him to be a day later, but was actually seven years to the day, a strange thing happened in the sky. He watched the light gradually fade and a dark circle crept across the sun. When the earth became as dark as night he turned away with a strange sense of foreboding and stumbled. His hand touched a cold object, and when he raised it, he saw that it was a horseshoe. Now we know that iron or salt keep the fairy bewitchments away, and it was a strange stroke of fate that his hand fell on a horseshoe. When the sun's light returned he was still grasping the horseshoe, and he was standing at the hollow of the hill near his house.

He walked down to the farm, wanting to get it ready for Kate coming home. Little did he know that he had links in the Other World for he had no recollection of what had happened to him. Sure, isn't that the way it is with the fairies, their time is not the same as ours.

When he reached his house everything looked different. He peered in the window and there was his wife Kate, putting a scone on the griddle. When she moved back he saw a man sitting on Hugh's own chair, rocking a cradle by his side, and in it was a baby. Hugh pushed on the door and knocked and pushed again but it wouldn't budge an inch to his pushes. When his wife finally opened it he could only stare at her, so beautiful was she that he wanted to pull her into his arms and never let her go.

'What do you want, old man?' she asked. He opened his eyes wide in shock.

'Kate, don't you know me? I'm your husband, come back.'

'Away with you, old man. You're not my husband. He was the most handsome man in these parts. Look at you, you wizened, filthy man! Away with you!'

She moved to shut the door on him and he caught a glimpse of himself in the mirror opposite. She was indeed right. The face that looked back at him was old and wrinkled with a grey tangled beard that hung to his waist.

But worst of all, behind him shimmered the image of the *Leannan Sidhe*, as beautiful as before. Her eyes beguiled him again and she pulled him away and that was the last that was seen of the two of them forever.

And Kate had had to stand the brunt of her father's anger when he opened the bag of gold and found only the withered leaves of the buttercups in place of the gold that was left. He maintained that Hugh had stolen it back and had run off, for Kate's father was not a man who believed in the fairies.

Shiela Quigley was one of the great storytellers of Ireland and this is a version of one of her stories.

26

BIDDY RUA AND THE POTEEN MAKERS

Sure, it isn't a strange thing at all that people in the olden days believed in spirits, ghosts and fairies, because the world of spirits was all around them. The banshees foretold deaths, and the souls of the dead hovered in the same place where they had lived their lives. Fairies lived in every hill and glen, and if you believed in them, they kept in touch with you and the other humans who needed a helping hand, and betimes the fairies were better to people than some of their own kith and kin. The general feeling was 'If you are good to them, then they'll return the kindness one hundredfold,' especially when the devil was all the time watching out for human weakness.

Now, that's an important thing to keep in mind, for there are those who will try to tell you that all spirits and fairies are bad, some are, but most aren't. It's not so strange that Other World beings weren't visible in the daytime when people were hard at work, but at night, when human hands were idle, the whole spirit world became fully active. In the gloom of the winter evenings from Halloween on, lonely hills and empty roads were spots to be avoided, for at times like that the fairies and spirits with ill-will towards humans would come out. Only the foolhardy or the ne'er-do-wells went abroad to such places. But the cover of darkness had its rewards, for night time was a perfect time to be about illegal ventures like making poteen, the other kind of spirit that warms the heart and eases the mind.

Johnny O'Kane and Eamon McCluskey of South Derry had a wee poteen still going at a lonely spot at the bottom of Slieve Gallion. They felt safe enough because the police didn't venture too far into the mountain. When the distilling was finished and poteen was ready they sat down to have a sip of it. Just to test it, mind!

Sure, the moon came out from behind the clouds and there, standing right in front of them, was a wee red-haired woman of uncertain age. Now, you would think that they would be surprised, but they weren't because they knew her to be one of Gráinne Rua's fairies sent to help them. Gráinne Rua, the banshee of the O'Cathan clan, still looked after her own, but when a death wasn't imminent she sent one of the fairies, lest people might be afraid. These fairies were good, and the men had no fear of the one standing in front of them. They gave her a wee dram of poteen and she nodded her approval.

Then she handed the glass back and spoke in Irish. '*Is maith liom potín mar shin ach bí curamac, tá na pólíní ag teacht anocht*' (I like poteen like that but be careful, the police are coming tonight). Then she disappeared into the darkness.

Johnny and Eamon hurriedly hid all the apparatus and, each with a keg of poteen on his shoulder, zigzagged up the mountain. When they reached a safe place behind the rocks they lay flat and looked down to see if what the fairy had said was true. In a couple of minutes, as sure as they were stone cold sober, there they saw two revenue men and two stout policemen puffing their way up the hill to the place where they had set up their still just a ween of hours before. Didn't those police and revenue men start searching? Every tuft of grass was kicked and poked with their sticks, but Johnny and Eamon were too wise in the ways of the police, and when the searchers voices carried up the mountain, their complaints set the two men sniggering and laughing.

'Wouldn't you think that the poteen men would leave us a wee tot to drink after all our exertions? The boys back at the station will be annoyed that they've been robbed of their wee drop.' After the police left in disgust the two men went home by a different route and met no one on the road.

When they reached Johnny's house his da was waiting up for his drop of poteen, for he was known to be the best 'taster' in the district. Johnny waited while his da swirled it around in his mouth and swallowed it.

'Good stuff,' was his da's report.

Only then did he tell his father about the fairy warning them. His da didn't answer, but just nodded sagely and took a puff on his clay pipe. He took another mouthful of poteen and nodded his head, again without saying a word.

'Da, did you ever see her?' asked Johnny, a mite impatient that his da would be too drunk to answer if he kept on drinking.

'Aye, many a time. That's Biddy Rua, the fairy woman of the O'Cahans. She was there to warn you just as she warned me when I was at the making of poteen. She enjoys a wee drop herself, so I hope you obliged.'

'We did Da, and she thought it was good stuff too.'

'Aye, boys keep at it and someday ye'll be as good as me.'

The men smiled at each other and the old man started talking. They knew they were in for a night of yarns, for once his da got a few glasses in him he got the urge to talk about the old times.

'… and I have to say that she saved me many a time from the police.' When the old man's voice descended into a mumble followed by a snore Johnny and Eamon slipped quietly out. The next day they knew how very lucky they'd been because the news went quickly around the country that a whole lot of men had been arrested and put in Derry Jail for the heinous offence of 'making moonshine'.

27

THE WHISKEY SMUGGLERS AND THE FAIRIES

It's no secret the sort of things that happen around the coast of Ireland, and the north coast in particular was famous for the smuggling that went on.

There was a boat moored off Magilligan Point and it was discharging kegs of whiskey to the smugglers who were waiting on the beach. When the kegs were brought ashore two of the smugglers, Billy and Ned, tied the kegs across the saddles of their horses and then mounted the horses themselves. That was some weight for each horse to be carrying but sure, the smugglers weren't too concerned, as long as they brought the whiskey to the tavern that had promised to buy it.

Off they trotted at a brisk pace, but not long after that they heard the faint sounds of horses' hooves behind them. Now, they thought that they were alone on the lonely road and surmised that the only other people who could be abroad at that time must be the Revenue Men. Everyone knew that if they caught you with smuggled goods, sure, they would claim it and dispose of it and you would be marched off to jail. Some were even heard to say these men made more than their wages by selling off seized goods. Imagine that, taking away the good character of the revenue men. Tut-tut.

Anyway, they began to push their horses on, which was a bit dangerous, seeing that they had two heavy kegs each to carry. They whipped up their horses into a gallop, but no matter how fast they went the sounds got closer. Eventually, Ned dropped back, for his horse was tiring, but he managed to hide behind a hedge. The pursuing horses surged on by without even a look in his direction, but the other man, Billy, was a very thran and stubborn person.

He thought to himself, 'I have the fastest horse in the whole county, there's none have the beat of him, and we can outrun any other beast.' So he pushed on, slapping the horse's rump and trying to hold onto the kegs that were growing heavier by the minute on the poor animal's back. But still Billy didn't give up, and he continued till the horse was glistening with sweat and foaming at the mouth.

Eventually he saw that he'd have to choose between the whiskey and the horse, and he dumped the kegs. With the weight of the whiskey gone, his horse flew like a bird across the fields, and jumped hedges with Billy spurring him on, in an effort to shake off his pursuers, but without success. When the crashing sound of the other horses' hooves were almost upon him he pulled his mount to a stop, jumped down and turned, ready to fight the revenue men.

He looked and waited but there wasn't hair nor sight of anyone, but the sound of approaching hooves was almost deafening. There may not have been anything to see, but Billy felt a great blast of air and a shout as the invisible horses passed by.

'That was a great race you ran, Billy boy and that's a fine mount you have there. Away and find your kegs, for your friend has them safe and sound.'

It was then that Billy knew for certain that it was the Pooka fairies that had chased him. Sure, weren't they were known to have a mischievous way with them at times, and many a song has been written about them.

> While the Pooka horse holds his frantic course
> O'er wood and mountain fall,
> And the Banshee's croon, a rhythmic rime
> From the crumbling, ivied wall.

When Billy retraced his course he found his companion lying at his ease on a bank of soft moss, with his mouth under the tap of a keg, having a drink. Billy started laughing at the way they'd been deceived and the two of them drank their fill. Before the morning rays rose in the east they loaded the kegs on the horses and set off.

Now, wasn't Billy still glad that no earthly horse had outrun his and he was still able to claim that his was the fastest beast in the country?

Whether that was the whiskey talking or not, we don't know but you can be sure that they were more careful with the smuggling from then on.

28

BLINKING THE CATTLE

As you probably know, a cow is a very valuable animal to any small farm and could mean the difference between starvation and plenty for the family that depends on it. With that being the case, every farmer looking after his cattle made sure that there was enough grass in the field in summer and enough fodder for winter.

In County Derry a farmer was at a loss to know why his cattle were not thriving and why the cows' milk was failing. There was no good reason that he could see. Indeed, he even stayed up at night to make sure that no more harm could come to them because he had some inkling that there was magic afoot, though whether it was from the 'wee folk' or the '*Sluagh*' (spirits of the restless dead) he wasn't certain. Sure, it is well known that the magic they used was the 'blink'. Now, the 'blink' had a bad effect on any person, place or thing that the fairies didn't like, and there were some people who were able to call it up at the drop of a hat and you wouldn't be knowing who did the calling.

Night after night, the farmer stayed near the barn, and day-by-day he watched the fields, until the man was nearly dead on his feet, but still there was no explanation. His wife was beginning to think that her husband was mad, so she suggested they send for Joe Tate, a witch doctor around the Dunboe parish, who was a man well versed in curing the 'blinking' of cattle. Well, he came to the farm and looked around, checked out the cattle and the byre where they did the milking. When he went into the house he asked the farmer's wife a question,

'Did anybody borrow something made of metal from you recently?'

'Aye,' she answered, 'My neighbour borrowed my griddle pan.'

'Is she involved with the Devil?'

'God save us, no,' said the farmer's wife, 'what are ye saying? She's a very upright woman, and I know she'll bring it back when she's finished with it.'

Tate seemed very sceptical and said that he would put a spell on it. 'If she's involved with the wan below, the griddle pan will soon tell us. If not, then she'll keep it until she's finished with it.'

In two shakes of a lamb's tail there was a knock at the door. The woman was standing outside with the griddle pan, complaining that every time she hung the griddle pan on the crook over the fire the flames leapt and burnt at her fingers and ran up her arm.

'Take the blessed thing back,' she said 'and never let me borrow anything from this house again.'

Sure, from the second that the griddle pan left that woman's hands the 'blinking' stopped and the cattle were on the mend. Joe had saved the day once more.

29

BLINKING THE CHURN

Joe Tate would seem to have been a very busy man around the Dunboe area, disposing of the 'blink', for wasn't another woman having a terrible time trying to get butter from her churn. She tried everything, but no matter what she tried the milk wouldn't thicken and no butter would come. The milk would splash around and she nearly broke the arm off herself trying to turn the churn handle, but narry a bit of butter came out. All she was left with was the sour milk.

Although she didn't believe in the 'blink' herself, when she met the farmer's wife in the market and heard how his cattle were cured she decided that she had nothing to lose. She made sure to tell Joe Tate when he came that she wasn't a believer in magic, being a strict good living Christian.

'As I am myself, Missus, but if the good Lord gave me the gift of curing the "blink", then I'm going to use it. Now, let me see that churn.'

He had a good look at the churn, inside and out and muttered to himself that he knew who the culprit was, but he wasn't going to enlighten the woman until he had the evidence to prove it.

'Now,' he said to the woman, 'I need a well-worn horseshoe, two of your hat-pins and seven nails with not a speck of rust on them. While you're getting them for me, hand me a bucket and point me in the direction of a stream.'

The woman did so and Joe went to the stream. Luckily it was south-running because a north-running one would have been useless for curing the 'blink'. When he went back into the house, all the things he needed were laid out neatly on the table.

He counted them very carefully and then proceeded to close all the doors and windows. The woman was standing there, fidgeting with her apron, not knowing what the man was about and thinking that she had made a mistake calling him in.

He poked up the fire, and in the pot he placed the iron things and poured the water over them, and then he hung it on the crook. Within a couple of minutes, and with a wee bit more poking and hoking at the fire, the water began to boil, and, just at that moment, didn't the woman see a neighbour passing the window? She rose to go and unlock the door, but Joe warned her not to move.

'That's just what I expected,' he said.

Well, that man knocked and knocked, and the poor woman nearly had to be held down on the chair to stop her opening the door. When the pot boiled over she heard the man scream out in agony.

'What are you doing woman? Take that pot off the fire because the pins are stabbing my heart?'

Sure, the poor woman didn't know what was going on and went again to open the door, but Joe stopped her.

'Let him have his cure,' he said, stirring the pot again. ''Tis what's needed if you're to have any butter.'

The man screamed even louder. 'For the love of God, I'm done with blinking Missus.'

Joe lifted the pot off and poured the scalding water over the churn. When the woman looked out the window she saw the tails of her neighbour's coat flapping in the wind. He left Dunboe soon after and was never seen around those parts again. Would you believe that from that day on the woman had the creamiest golden butter in the district and Joe was the first to get from each new batch, for without him she never would have had the butter to give.

30

JOHN AND THE
FAIRY TREE

There was a man called John McLaughlin who lived near Coleraine in County Derry and the poor man was nearly going mad because of all the strange things that were happening around his farm and house. It was the year 1907 and all was going well with him until his chimney started to give him bother, with the wind pushing the smoke back into his kitchen.

'John,' said his wife, 'you'll have to do something about that smoke for it's blinding me, I can hardly see the pictures on the wall at all for the thickness of it.'

'Houl' your whist, woman,' says John, 'a wee bit o' smoke won't do ye any harm.'

'Well, if you're not of a mind to do it, I'll do it meself!' said she and walked out the back door.

Well, John heard her hacking away at something and when he went out, there she was trying to cut a branch off the rowan tree.

'Ye've dropped more leaves than ye'll have left,' said John. 'Gimme that saw, and I'll cut a decent bush for a chimney cleaning.'

Well now, he took a spade and went to a holly bush, beyond the midden. Just when he was about to dig it up he heared Mickey, his neighbour, calling.

'Ah, John, I wouldn't be doing that if I was you, sure, that bush is the favourite meeting place of the fairies and they'll be coming after ye if ye disturb it.'

John looked at his wife, for he was in two minds now about what to do.

'Go ahead, man, that's nowt but an 'oul tale and there's no such things as fairies.'

John took another look at his wife's face and it was as sour as last week's buttermilk. If it was a choice between listening to neighbourly advice and living with a sour puss he knew which one to choose. He started to dig, and weren't his arms as sore as could be that night.

The next morning, when the fire was dead in the hearth, he pushed the branch up the chimney, and a powerful lot of soot came falling down. His wife was tut-tutting about the mess but John wasn't going to stop in the middle of what he was doing.

'Would ye get out of me way, woman dear, and let me get on with it. Ye wanted it cleaned now ye're getting it. Away and feed the hens or milk the cow 'til I finish.'

When he'd dislodged as much soot as he could, he shovelled it all up and took it out to the garden at the back of his house and buried it in the big hole that was left when he dug up the holly bush. He came back into the house, sure, his wife spoke not a word of thanks or the like for she was busy cleaning the dust away from the cups and bowls on the dresser.

That night the fire burned well and there was no smoke blowing down the chimney, and his wife seemed well pleased. She made him a barmbrack loaf filled with raisins and cherries and lathered it with creamy fresh butter as a special treat. She was smiling when she handed it to him with a big bowl of tea. Truth to tell, John didn't know where to look, for t'was seldom that he saw a smile crack his wife's face.

'I have to give it to ye John, ye did a fine job,' she said, banking up the fire and covering it with turf ash to keep it live for the morning.

Next morning, a powerful screech from his Martha had John jumping up out of bed and running into the kitchen, for he thought someone had come in and attacked her with an axe. But what was she doing? Only standing back by the door, pointing at the fireplace, and there was the soot that John had buried, laying all over the front of the hearth and beyond.

'Begod,' said he, 'what did ye do Martha?'

'What did I do?' she screamed. 'Nothin! What did you do, ye big eejit?'

'Houl' your whist, woman,' said John, and he pulled on a coat over his nightshirt and went out to the garden. There he saw a big hole where he had buried the soot and it was empty. He went back inside and calmed his wife.

'Somebody's playing a trick on us, Martha. It must be that Mickey. I'll go and see him.'

He dressed and presented himself at Mickey's door. When his neighbour came out, John lost no time in telling him off about digging up the soot.

'God's truth, John, I'd never do anything like that. I'm telling ye. It's the fairies. Mark my words, because I know for a fact that that holly bush is their place.'

John marched off home thinking his neighbour's head was 'away with the fairies'. He said no more to Martha than to state that it wasn't Mickey's doing and he set about burying the soot again while herself set about washing and cleaning the mess. Just to make sure the soot wouldn't up and away into the house again he put a big rock over the hole and told himself that that was the end of that. But it wasn't.

The very next morning the soot was in the kitchen again, spread all over her lovely blue dresser and curdled in the milk churn and the black soot was even stirred right into the butter she'd spent hours making.

She began to sob. 'Oh John, what'll we do?'

'Nothing,' he answered, 'I'll not let something like this beat me, for I don't believe in fairies and I'll find out who's doing this.'

No sooner were the words out of his mouth but a shower of soot sprayed all over the lovely whitewashed outside walls, and stones flew in from the field and jigged around in mid-air, nearly hitting Martha. John shut the door with a bang, but would you believe that a stone as big as a boulder came right through the door, turned around in mid-air and smashed its way out again through the window? John grabbed Martha by the arm and rushed out into

the street, and the ruckus from inside the house was so deafening
that the neighbours came running and stood in the street listening
to the commotion.

Well, that night a few of the men gathered in Mickey's house,
for that's where John and Martha were staying for the next few
days because as sure as the devil will take my soul if I tell a lie,
Martha's house was ruined.

'What ye need to do, John, is get another tree and plant it in the
exact same spot, for you stole their house and now they've stolen yours.'

'Aye,' piped up another neighbour, 'it's tit-for-tat, so it is.'

Mickey said, 'There's a holly tree up thon lane and I know for a fact
that t'isn't the fairies'. What d'ye say we go up there and dig up a wee
healthy wan and plant it in the hole and you put the soot elsewhere.'

'Righto,' said John. 'If it gets herself back into her house, I'm all
for it.'

The next day John and Mickey dug up a strong wee holly bush
and brought it back. They manured the ground well and stuck in
the tree and before they went back to Mickey's, he said, 'John, ye
have to say you're sorry and tell them they'll be safe on your land.'

'Ach, Mickey, sure I'd feel a bit of a fool doing that.'

'No more'n they would if ye plant a tree and don't say it, for
that's the purpose. You're putting it back 'cos you're sorry you took
it away in the first place!'

So John stood, feeling like a right eijit, and told the fairies he
was sorry and they'd be welcome to live on the land for as long as
they wanted, then, satisfied with their work they made their way
back to Mickey's.

'What do we do now,' enquired Martha.

'Just sit it out, Missus,' answered Mickey, 'for they'll not be
moving back till they know the tree's there for good.'

And every morning after that John watered the tree and Martha
peeked in the window of their house, and soon the clattering and
banging faded away as the holly tree took root.

Within a month they were able to move back in, and every day
John made a point of saluting the tree when he passed, and they
never had a bit of bother from that day to this.

31

NURSING A BABY THAT'S NOT OF MY OWN

There was a woman who lived on the west side of Donald's Hill in County Derry and she went by the name of Nancy. If the stories are to be believed, and they are, she was a handsome woman. She was tall, with fair skin as smooth as an eggshell. Her hair was glossy black and her eyes like a bright blue summer sky, and in them the loveliest twinkle you ever saw.

She went to the market one Monday and there she met a fine specimen of a man called Patrick. Didn't he recognise her from going to church in the next parish? And never before did he have the nerve to talk to her because her da was always in the vicinity. Sure, this day he plucked up his courage and went over to her, for she was on her lone.

'You're Nancy McCluskey, aren't you?'

She looked up and saw a very tall man, much taller than she, and this was the first time that she had ever met a man that she could look up to, her being so tall herself. Well, the young couple chatted and walked around the market together, and when it came time to go home he asked if they could walk together. They chatted that much that their feet ate up the miles, and before they parted at her gate they set to see each other to dance at the crossroads on Saturday.

In less than twelve months they were married and half the country came to their wedding, for Nancy and Patrick were very well thought of. The revelry went on till the wee small hours and everybody agreed that they were a couple that the sun shone on.

Barely a year later they had a lovely wee baby, with hair as fair as its mother's was black and she was the apple of their eyes. There was nothing that Nancy liked more than sitting in the rocking chair feeding her baby, and a fine nurse she was with a very contented baby. As was the way with the neighbours in a country place, they came and went and all of them said what a treasure of a mother she was, remarking that there was no happier couple or sweeter baby in all of the land.

Now, it happened at that very same time that the queen of the fairies had a child about the same age, but the queen was sickly and wasn't able to feed it and the king was pure distracted when he saw his son failing and his wife worrying herself nearly to death. In desperation he sent his fairies out to find out if there was a woman nursing her baby who could wet-nurse his. The gentry, for that was what the little people were called by humans, went far and wide, and then they heard about this lovely woman called Nancy. They went to the house and watched but there was only one thing, Nancy was well protected from the wee folk and they couldn't get near her at all. You see, Nancy always wore a charm around her neck, and sewn up in her skirt was a herb and a bit of burnt soil from the bonfire on St John's Eve to ward off the fairies and prevent them from leaving a changeling in wee Ellen's place.

Sure, all babies start to teethe and get a bit fretful, and one night her wee baby didn't settle at all. Not bothering to put on her skirt, for she was wearing a nightgown, Nancy went down to the kitchen to get a rub for her baby's gums, for what mother could bear to see her child suffer. She was humming to herself, and as soon as she opened the door to the kitchen, didn't three of the fairies grab her, and before she could bless herself and touch the charm around her neck, the gentry dragged her away.

When she tried to call to her husband she couldn't find her voice. Gone it was, and didn't they sweep her outside and place her on a white horse? Didn't it gallop off through the night and there was no rider on it but herself? Now, wasn't that a strange thing because Nancy had never ever ridden a horse in her life, and even though she was filled with fear she did not fall off.

It was a beautiful night, just between dusk and dark, but she could see very clearly, and every place that she passed didn't she recognise them all? Every tree and every rock was known to her. But then, after a while she did not see any part of the country, for the night was as black as tar.

The horse stopped abruptly and someone standing beside it lifted her down with strong arms. When she looked around, wondering what part of the country she was in, all she saw was a big, big house surrounded by trees and guarded by a high golden gate which opened on its own.

'Glory be,' she thought, 'I've never seen anything like this before. Maybe I'm dreaming,' but somehow she knew she was not.

A fine-looking gentleman opened the door and took her arm, after bidding her *'Céad míle fáilte,'* as if he knew her and was expecting her, and he led her up the steps to the grand doorway. Her mouth opened in wonderment, for wasn't it the grandest hall anybody ever saw, for everything was bright and shining. 'Twas then that she got the feeling that there was something peculiar but, being a sensible girl, she kept her wits about her. He led her into an even wider marble hall with a huge fire burning in a towering fireplace.

Bowing to her, he said, 'Won't you excuse me? The master will be with you in a moment.'

Nancy sat down, for what else was she to do and she in her night wear. Now there's the other thing, when she looked down she was no longer clothed in her nightdress. It was gone and she was wearing a lovely dress as yellow as the morning sun. And more, where her feet had been bare she had the softest white leather boots fitting her feet like gloves. She was content then that she was dreaming, for never in her life had she owned a dress nor boots as elegant as these.

She peeked around and saw a young woman standing at the doorway of a small room, looking at her with a very sad expression. Nancy felt a wee pull of sorrow, for it was as if the woman wanted to speak but wasn't sure of a welcome. Nancy, being a friendly woman, bade her time of day. The woman cast a glance over her shoulder and then walked towards Nancy until she was right beside her. She bent down and whispered.

'Take my advice Nancy, and take neither bite nor sup while you are in this house, for if you do you'll not set eyes on your baby or husband again! I ate and drank my fill when they brought me here and I have only a bitter sorrow to show for it.'

'How did you know my name?' asked Nancy.

'This is an enchanted place, the home of the king of the fairies, and they will not let you go for everything here is bewitched, even the food and water. Remember, not a sip or you will be lost here like me.'

'What can I do for you?' asked Nancy, her kindly feelings showing.

'My husband is Dan Scullion from over by Bovey. Ask him to have the priest say this prayer and *Buíochas le Dia*, I, Mary, will return to him and my baby.' She pressed a piece of paper into Nancy's hand and Nancy slipped it into her boot.

Before Nancy could ask another question the woman was gone and a man dressed like a king came into the hall, followed by the same young woman carrying a baby. The man took the baby and handed it to Nancy and motioned to her to put it to her breast. The baby sucked hungrily, and when it had taken its fill his eyes closed in sleep. The man dismissed the young woman and took the baby.

'Follow me,' he said and walked before her into another room. There, sitting in a beautiful chair, bedecked in the finest clothes, was a lovely lady that he introduced as 'My Queen'.

'You are most welcome,' said the queen, 'I thank you for feeding my baby but now, please, you must have some repast,' she said, indicating a table beside her, filled with the most delectable cakes and food Nancy had ever seen. Even though her stomach was grumbling for the want of it she declined, bearing in mind what the young woman had said.

'I thank you, your Majesty, I am not hungry.'

'How can I repay you if you won't eat?' asked the queen. Nancy paused and thought, then said, 'You can help me in one way. I ask you for a cure for my mother, who has the sorrows since my father died.'

'Since I was the cause of your coming here, you shall have the cure. Go home and pull ten green rushes from the side of the river, throw the tenth away and squeeze the juice of the rest of them into a cup. Give this to your mother to drink and in seven days she will be well.'

The king, for that is who the man was, took a ring from his own finger and put it on hers. 'Take this,' he said,' and do not lose it, for it will protect you from all harm.'

He took a small phial of ointment and rubbed it on her eyes and immediately she found herself in a very dark place at the end of which was a door with the light shining around the edges.

'Do not be afraid,' he said, 'you are not far from your home,' and he led her towards the door. 'The moon will show you the way.'

She looked up, and when she turned around he was gone and she was standing on the hill behind her house. As she walked towards it the gloom of the parting night softened and not a breath of air did she feel on her face. In the cottage she slipped into the bedroom again, and there her baby was lying contented as a lamb and her husband was still asleep.

If it weren't for the fact that she had on her feet the finest pair of boots, she would have believed that she had just woken from a dream. With a start she remembered the lovely young woman in the enchanted palace. She felt inside the boot and took out the paper and tucked it under her pillow. She blessed herself and slid into bed, snuggled into the warmth of her husband and closed her eyes.

'Tomorrow,' she told herself before she went asleep, 'I will visit the priest and tell him about Mary and her husband. Then I'll go to see my mother.'

32

BROGEY MCDAID AND THE WEE FOLK

Now, you might have heard the likes of this story before but I'm sure there have been some changes in the telling because my great-aunt told me that it was the honest truth. All I can do is pass on what my great-grandfather said when he told it to my great-aunt. Since neither is around to dispute it, I'll relate what I remember, for I was just about twelve years of age when I first heard it and reality and fantasy sometimes merge.

> Ah, these forty long years I have travelled
> All by the contents of me pack.
> Me hammers, me awls and me pincers
> I carry them all on me back.

(From 'The Cobbler')

There was a journeyman shoemaker who travelled around the country making shoes, and it was a bitterly cold day just before Christmas 1830 when Paddy Joe McDaid, nicknamed 'Brogey', (after the Irish word for 'shoe', '*brogue*') arrived in a wee place a few miles outside of Derry. Journeymen of all kinds relied on the people to give them lodgings. Sure, it was the tradition in the country areas never to refuse a bed to anyone.

This man knocked on the door of a nice wee cottage and when Maggie McLaughlin opened the door it's no word of a lie that his heart leapt and it was nearly like a blow to his chest, for she was the loveliest girl he had ever laid eyes upon.

'Come in out of the cold,' said she. ''Tis a bitter day.'

He needed no second bidding, and didn't she offer him a place beside the hearth in front of a big turf fire with a sup o' tea and a lump of soda scone in his hand.

'Take off your boots, if ye have a mind to,' said she, 'for it's wet through they must be with all that tramping the byways.'

When Matt, her father, came in from the barn, Brogey and Maggie were getting on like candle wax and a wick and Matt was right glad to see the smile on his daughter's face, for she was getting on for thirty and no man on the horizon. He nodded to himself too, since Maggie had never invited a man to shed his shoes before. It was for that reason that he gave Brogey a mighty shake of the hand and chatted with him while Maggie put out the supper.

Now, Brogey was an honest man and he saw that the soles were hanging off Matt's boots, so he offered to fix them for him by way of thanking Maggie. For poor folk didn't have the money to spend on boots, and half the childer in the country were running around in their bare feet anyway.

It must have been love that made Brogey settle down, for he never moved on, and wasn't he right glad during the hard winter that his time tramping as a journeyman shoemaker was over. He and Maggie made plans to tie the knot as soon as Lent was over. And what a wedding it was! Matt sent out word to the whole townland and not a one refused except the 'oul skinflint of a cobbler from over the hill. Sure, they weren't a bit surprised, for the man must have heard about Brogey's great skills, and he was afeard he might set up and do him out of the little bit of business that there was.

Matt moved to the lower room and Maggie and her man had the upper room in the house to themselves. The two men worked together companionably and fixed up a place in a wee room attached to the house for Brogey to start a shoemaker's shop.

'Maybe you could even make saddles, bridles and the like for you're a talented man with the leather,' said Maggie's father, 'and sure, if the trappings for the horse fail we're a bit stuck to have them fixed,

for that cobbler doesn't know one end of a horse from the other.'
Mind you, that cobbler made some sort of shape at mending the
boots for the local farmers, but he wasn't good enough for the gentry
who went to Derry or Coleraine for their footwear.

Now, Brogey took great pride in his work, but it's hard for a
man to start up and attract customers at the beginning. Soon
though his expertise was broadcast around the countryside. 'Sure,
he can make a pair of boots from scratch as well as fix up your
auld ones!' was the news. No matter what kind of shoe or boot
a man, woman or child wanted, Brogey could make it. The local
women were delighted, because on the *ceilidhe* nights it was the
custom to dress up, and a nice pair of shoes added class to the
outfit. The men began to notice that the soles of their boots
lasted longer too because he used only the best of leather. After
a while, some of the gentry came to have their shoes and boots
made too.

The cobbler began to lose business, for not only was he not
good at his trade but he was an auld crabbit man who was often
the worse for wear through his drinking of the porter, and would
as soon eat the nose off anyone who complained as look at them.

Everything was going grand for the young couple until one
night Brogey's workshop went on fire and he and his wife Maggie
were lucky that it didn't spread to the house. The locals gathered
around and formed a bucket chain, and soon the fire was put out
but the shoemaker's room was burnt out and the leather unusable.
Only the iron lasts on which he fashioned the shoes and nailed
them together were saved. Maggie was distraught, for wasn't she
expecting their first baby? I have to say that there were rumours
flying around about the cause of the fire, but as Brogey said,
'What's done is done and nothing will change it.'

'Sometimes' my grandfather said, 'an ill-wind blows something
good, for didn't the people around set to and built a place onto the
house for Brogey to carry on his business? And it was much better
than the wee room he had before, for hadn't it a grand big window
facing the road so people could see the lovely work he did. There
was only one thing wrong, they didn't have the money to buy the

quality of leather that he wanted, and the cobbler wasn't about to let him have any of his.'

Brogey went to bed that night, keeping his worries to himself, but he couldn't sleep. He got up and made his way into the workroom and looked around. All he could find were some small pieces of leather in a bag, and to pass the time he made up a wee pair of shoes. Sure, doing a good job, even if it's on tiny shoes that would fit no one, gave him some satisfaction, so he set to and made another pair. Both pairs were too small for even the tiniest feet, but he was satisfied that he had little shoes to put on display to show off his skill. He put them neatly together and admired his own work, knowing that the shoes had been fashioned without the use of even one nail. For some strange reason his worries had gone and he was ready to do whatever it took to earn a living for Maggie, himself and the baby. He went back to bed and slept like a man with no concerns.

It seemed as if he'd only been asleep for moments when he was shook awake, 'Brogey, Brogey, wake up. Come and see what's in your room.'

He dragged himself out of bed and followed his wife out to the workroom. When she opened the door he couldn't believe his eyes. There, sitting on the table was one of the nicest hides of Moroccan goat leather that he had ever seen. He touched it, felt it and even smelled it and he knew that he had never seen the quality of it before.

'Maggie,' he said, his voice almost breaking with emotion, 'we have the best neighbours that God could give a man. Now we'll go and thank them, for this is the best day of our lives.'

They went to the first neighbour, but he didn't know what they were talking about.

'Sure I didn't do that, Brogey. I would have if I'd had the money but I didn't. Maybe it was Barney,' he said.

The couple went to Barney, but he knew nothing either and sent them on to another, but no one seemed to know anything about it. Puzzled, they walked back to the house and when Brogey went into the room again he noticed the two pairs of tiny shoes were gone.

'Maggie,' he called, 'did you move two wee pairs of shoes I made?'

'Indeed I didn't. Sure, I don't interfere with your work, Brogey,' she answered, and went on making the breakfast.

It wasn't long before people started to come into the shop to ask Brogey about the leather. Soon a bit of a crowd gathered, and the talk went round and round, but it was only when he mentioned about the wee shoes that they looked at one another.

'Sure, if it wasn't one of us it must have been the fairies,' Matt said, and that was the general consensus. 'Imagine fairies coming to help out,' they were saying with excited, babbling voices.

'What you need to do,' said Barney, rubbing his chin and stretching his neck, 'is make another wee pair or two to thank them and leave them here on the table, and if it was them then they'll be back.'

With that they all left and Maggie looked at her husband. 'D'you believe all that nonsense?' she said.

'Well now, Maggie, maybe it's not nonsense but if it is all I'm out is a few wee bits of leather.'

Maggie tut-tutted and left him to work. All day he cut and sewed and never put an iron nail near the tiny shoes, for fairies don't like iron at all, and he did the finest job he'd ever done in his life. He examined them and couldn't find a flaw anywhere.

'Ah,' he thought, 'I could do the same work on other shoes if I had enough leather and I'd be the happiest man in the world.' Before the words were fully out of his mouth he had the strongest desire to cut out the makings of a shoe from the new goatskin. He smoothed it out on the table, felt it for thicker parts that needed skiving but he had no need to spend time on that, for it was the smoothest leather he'd ever felt. By the time Maggie called him in for his dinner he had the first lady's shoe made and oh boyo, it was grand! Right after his meal he went back to the work-room, and by the time he'd finished it was nearly midnight but on his window shelf he placed the most beautiful pair of moss green leather shoes ever seen in the country, if he wasn't mistaken.

That night he slept like a baby with a full stomach, and in the morning he couldn't wait to see if the wee shoes were gone.

He rushed into the workroom and on the bench was another beautiful skin of leather in a rich dark brown. He searched around the bench but the little shoes were gone.

'So it was the fairies! I knew it!' He held the leather to his nose to inhale its rich smell, and there underneath, on the table, was a tiny bell. When he lifted it, it rang with a sweet, tiny tinkle and begod when he looked up a lady had just entered the shop.

'I couldn't help but see those beautiful shoes in your window. May I try them on please?'

He turned his back while the lady slipped off her boot and tried on the first shoe, for a man doesn't look at a lady's ankle. 'Oh, the other one please, this fits like a glove!' A few moments later, when he turned around, she was walking the length of the shop with the moss-green shoes on her tiny feet.

'Oh, sir, these are exquisite. I must have them. I must! I simply must!'

Sure the bell tinkled again and another lady came in. Her face fell in disappointment when she saw the shoes on the first lady's feet.

'Oh, I so wanted those lovely shoes. I'll pay you more. How much are they?'

Before he could answer, the first lady said, 'Ten guineas, sir and they're mine.'

'I'll give you fifteen!'

'Twenty!'

'Twenty-five!' The bargaining went on and he stood there with his mouth agape.

At fifty guineas he held up his hand. 'Ladies, I will make another pair, slightly different of course, so you will both be satisfied.' He pondered about accepting the price but Maggie, on hearing the commotion had come up behind him.

'Fifty guineas it is,' she said and accepted the gold coins.
When they left he turned to his wife. 'That's a desperate high amount to pay for a pair of shoes,' he protested.

'Sure they can well afford it and don't forget that all our neighbours gave from their substance when they helped us, because none of them have much in their pockets. So we can share our good fortune, for without them and your good work we wouldn't have any.'

The pattern continued and ladies came and went, each buying shoes and passing on praise by word of mouth. The men followed the example and it seemed that every gentleman in the county was wearing high boots, made of the finest pigskin or goatskin. When a baby boy was born to Maggie, Brogey thanked God, for life couldn't be any better. But he began to have niggles of conscience about so much good fortune coming their way and not spreading it around as much as they should. Brogey, being an honest man, sat talking to Maggie one night after the baby went to sleep. He broached a subject that was giving him the tingles of guilt.

'Maggie, my love,' he started, 'I've had all this good fortune and I was passing by wee Jack's cobbler shop and it looked awful run down. You know I never meant to put him out of business, but that's the way it looked. I'm of a mind, and I hope you'll agree with me, that maybe I should go to him and offer him a goodly amount of money to let me buy over the business.'

Maggie looked up from her knitting but didn't say anything for a moment. She looked a bit anxious. 'Well, what do you think?'

'I think you are a good man and I'm a lucky woman. We've more than enough to do what's right. So go tomorrow and do what you've said. Now come on to bed.'

That night about midnight, he made his way to the workroom and what did he see but one of the wee folk sitting on his table trying on the tiny shoes that he made every day. He wasn't a bit shy and he sat down at his workbench and watched him without saying a word.

'You'll be thinking that it's time our swapping came to an end, aren't you?' said the wee man, stroking his beard and looking at him with sparkling eyes.

'Aye, along those lines, I was,' Brogey answered.

'Well, sir, let me put it like this. You've shoed every man, woman and child in this fairy kingdom, and right glad we are for you're the only man who made us shoes without nails. For you know that the iron isn't a good omen for us and that's a fact. We'll go now, but we'll make you a promise afore that. If you ever need help for yourself, your family or your neighbours, just leave your window ajar and we'll come. And if we need more shoes we'll let you know too.'

Brogey nodded. 'I don't know how to thank you. You've made us all very, very happy and we'll not forget it.'

'What goes around comes around,' said the wee man, 'Ah, would you look at that?' He pointed to the wall and Brogey looked up and saw nothing. When he lowered his eyes again the fairy was gone, and on the bench was a pile of beautiful leather skins of all colours, enough to last him for his time.

Now, you'll be wondering if he ever saw the fairy again, and sure he did. He needed their help again after the night of the Big Wind on 6 January 1839 but that's another story for another time.

And that's the story as my great-aunt told it to me and just as I told it to my children. Sure, how are they to know about the wee folk if we don't tell them?

33

Pauric and
the Fairies

*This is one of the stories handed down in the family and
embellished through the telling. It was never the same twice over.*

Once upon a time, and a long time ago it was, there was a wee
fellow who was always dobbin[1] school. He thought he was hard-
done-by if he didn't have at least one day off every week, and when
he did come back to school he had the greatest excuses for the
master. So good were they that the master never could get too
angry with him, for didn't his excuses make the master's day?

Now, the only reason I heard about Pauric was that my granda
was in the same class as him when he was a wee boy, and if the
truth be told my granda did more homework for Pauric than
Pauric ever did for himself. But then, my granda's mammy had a
soft spot for Pauric too, for hadn't he no mother to look after him,
her being dead when he was only a wean, as we say here.

Well, Pauric never carried a slate to school nor a bit of turf for
the stove because he had hardly the makings of a fire in his own
house, never mind taking turf to school. And nobody knew that
my great-granny slipped round to his house many a time with a
pot of dinner, for she couldn't bear the thought of weans[2] going
hungry for the want of food.

He was always acting the fool but sure, it was only his way of
not having to stand up in class and read, for he never got past the

third reader. Sure, we'd all try to help him when he would stumble or stutter over the words till he got red in the face. If he joked enough the master sent him to do a wee job, just so he could get on with the rest of the class's work.

Well, one day he came to school after a day's dobbin' and after the master called the roll he said, 'Where were you yesterday Pauric, we missed you?'

Sure, all the other scholars kept their heads down, writing their compositions and not daring to look at Pauric. They were afeard they might be caught with their ears sticking out to hear what the dobber might say for himself this time, and them all the while knowing there'd be a good story in it.

'Well master,' said Pauric, 'I was on my way here yesterday, bright and early, with a bit of turf in my pocket when it started teeming[3] down, and I had to run like the hare for shelter. I leapt over the March ditch and made for the bridge. An' that rain never gave over and there was me sitting there on a pile of stones, with the rain belting down and it making circles in the water. Sure, it was like a lullaby, and I fell asleep. By the time I woke up, master, it was time for going home. So I went.'

'Well,' said the master, 'you can start making up for some of the work that you missed by staying after school today.'

Now, Pauric wasn't the only one kept in that day, for didn't my granda forget to bring his slate, and the Master made him stay in to help improve his memory for the next day. Well, the master set them to work doing sums and went out, warning them not to copy and to have their work done by the time he came back. Pauric started scratching on the desk with his chalk, and it was getting on my granda's nerves for the noise of it was doing terrible things to his teeth.

'Will ye, for God's sake, count it in your head or on your fingers the way the master said. Ye'll have no chalk left at that rate o' goin',' said my granda.

'I'd rather scratch the desk than me head,' answered Pauric.

'Aye, well, since your head's as wooden as the desk, ye might as well,' said my granda.

'Here, if you help me with the hard ones I'll tell you what happened to me under the bridge yesterday.'

'The master said not to copy.'

Pauric was quick to answer, 'Sure he'll only know if we have the same wrong answer and you always get them right.'

With that Pauric gave a plaugher[4] and beat his chest. 'G'on,' he said, 'Sure, it was sitting in the rain that gave me this plaugher but it was worth it, for it's a wonder the thing that happened to me and ye'll never know it if I don't tell it to ye.'

Sure, the curiosity was too much for my granda, and he could bend the rules when it suited him. He called out the answers for Pauric to write down on the slate and Pauric pushed away his slate when the sums were done.

'Yesterday I got to singin' a wee song to myself, when I was sitting under the bridge,' said he, leaning back on the bench.

'Were you trying to frighten the fish out of the water?' sniggered my granda. (He still liked a wee bit of repartee, so he did.)

Pauric gave a snort. 'D'ye want to hear or not?' he demanded with a bit of temper.

'Alright, tell us what happened.'

'As I was saying, I was sitting under the bridge, humming a wee quiet tune to myself and looking at the rain making holes in the water, when a big salmon leapt in the air and I jumped. I mean, I never saw a salmon leap before, but then that's when it all happened!'

'What happened?' asked my granda, for Pauric had his attention now.

'All of a sudden the stone I was sitting on moved, and it slid from under me and I was falling down a big black hole. I was scared to death and shouting and screaming.' Pauric went quiet and sat back in his seat.

'And WHAT?' my granda was nearly mad with the curiosity again.

'Sure, I landed on my backside and I never found myself landing, so soft was it. When I took a look around, where was I but in the middle of the rath[5]? There was I with music and the sound of feet dancing and bright light all around and me trying not to be seen.'

'Were you're not frightened?' asked my granda.

'Devil the bit of me. Sure, the music was sweet so I knew there wouldn't be witches or knaves nearby, but I heard a bit of talking, so I sneaked in behind a tree, for I didn't want to scare whoever was there.'

'That was good of ye,' said my granda 'because if they saw a big gasur[6] like you walking in there, they'd be running away before you'd know it.'

'Sure, t'would put the heart jumpin' in them and there was a brave lot there when I peeped out from behind the tree. But, Seamus, you should have seen the way they could run up trees and down trees and still keep singing. I swear to God, I never saw the likes of it. Be Jaypers, they were dancing around, doing reels you never saw before, and slip jigs and things all around the ring, till the stones on the walls were nearly bouncing off.'

'Were they all dancing?'

'All except one wee fellow who couldn't get his feet to work together. He just couldn't keep time to the music and ye know, I couldn't stick it, because the others started laughing behind his back. Sure, I know what it's like to have people laugh at ye, so I started tapping my foot and clapping my hands and called out the one, two, threes, and would you believe he caught on? After that he started dancing better than all the others and he twirled the nicest wee fairy girl around that you ever saw in your life. And wasn't he as proud as could be, showing off to the others. Sure, if he'd been in the real world he would've stood ten feet tall, as it was, he towered over the others and him only one and a half feet off the ground.'

'So you taught one of the wee folk to dance? Imagine you teaching anybody anything. The master would be pleased about that.'

Pauric gave my granda a dour look and went on, 'Well, that's by the by,' he said, 'for didn't he come over, and he shook my hand and thanked me. And I'll have you know that he was the king of the fairies, and he said if I ever need help I just have to leave word under the bridge.'

'Maybe he'll give you a hand with your sums,' said my granda.

'Ach, houl' your whist, sure he means with important things like money and marrying the right girl and things like that.'

My granda turned away, not believing a word of it.

'Do you want to hear the end of it?' said Pauric.

'You mean there's more? You might as well finish it before the master comes back,' said my granda.

'Well, he grabbed me by the arm and pulled me into the ring to dance, and it was lively. I was near collapsing after an hour of prancing around and singing songs that I didn't even know I knew and the words escape me now. Well, they started playing another reel and two of them grabbed my hands and swung me round and round and round, getting faster and faster and we fell in a heap in the middle. I pulled myself up and where was I but back again, sitting under the bridge. D'ye know, I looked till the eyes sank in my head, but there wasn't a single stone I could move and I tried every one of them.'

'You're just coddin[6] as usual,' said my granda, 'You haven't a tune in your head, nor a boot to your foot, and you're trying to tell me that the king of the fairies was dancing and singing with ye?'

'As sure as I'm sittin' here,' said Pauric, crossing himself.

'Ye didn't happen to notice if that salmon was pulling on the line when you got back, did ye?' said my granda.

'Houl' yer whist,' said Pauric when the master came back in and told them they could go home.

Well, there's two ends to the story, and the first one is that my granda went across the fields to the bridge that evening and he tried to move the stones, but there wasn't the tiniest shift in any of them and all Pauric would say was that you probably had to sit on them in a certain way, and that was that.

And the second ending happened about twenty years after that, when a long Yankee car drew up outside my granda's house and a big tall man stepped out, dressed in a white suit and swinging a silver-topped cane. My granda came out and sure, didn't the big Yank pull him into a bear hug, nearly smothering him and lifting him off his feet.

'Don't you know me,' he shouted, 'I'm Pauric, come home!'

Later, when everything settled down, my granda listened while Pauric told him how the fairies had set him up with enough money to travel the world and start a business and now he was one of the richest men in America.

My granda half-believed him and went again under the bridge, but not a stone could he move, even an inch.

Maybe he didn't believe enough.

[1] *dobbin'*	*missing school*
[2] *weans*	*children – wee ones*
[3] *teeming*	*raining*
[4] *plaugher*	*chesty cough*
[5] *rath*	*circular earthen and stone fortification –*
	associated with the fairies
[6] *gasur*	*boy*
[7] *coddin'*	*joking*

34

LIG~NA~PAISTE (THE SERPENT IN THE POOL)

Sure, we all know that St Patrick raised his staff and ordered all the snakes in Ireland to gather around him. How he got rid of them is a matter of debate (and probably depends on how much you drank before the discussion began). Some say that he twirled them around the twisted top of his staff and flung them across the Irish Sea, over to what was then heathen England. Some say that he laid them out on a rock in Downpatrick and stepped on them before he threw them into the sea. Others say that he prayed and they shriveled up and died, and he just buried them where they lay. (Digging a hole big enough for all those snakes would have been a mighty hard piece of work.) Whatever the solution to the snake problem, what we do know is that one serpent, called Lig-na-Paiste, was overlooked.

I can tell you here and now that if you go to Banagher Forest, and a lovely place it is too, just follow the Owenreagh River to its source and you'll come to a small pool. This wee pool doesn't look anything out of the ordinary, but within its depths lies this terrible *paiste* (beast), as huge and fierce as any ever seen. After St Patrick died, didn't this brute of a snake come out and slither around the countryside, terrorising the people and ravishing the herds? It was said that it could swallow a whole cow at one go! It was a huge and fierce monster, for it had it the ability to exhale fire, which would make you think that it might have been half dragon and half snake. While he spent much of his time in the pool, Paiste would also curl around a green hill, and you wouldn't know it because he could change his colour till he was the same colour as the grass.

This was certainly no ordinary Paiste, indeed it wasn't, for this one was left over from the beginning of the world when God made all living creatures. There are those who say that this is the self-same one that was in the Garden of Eden, but I don't know about that.

The people around that wee corner of the county were in a desperate way with all this terrorising so they finally turned to St Murrough, a very holy man. Now, the saint knew that he couldn't put down the serpent on his own, so he fasted nine days and nights and prayed, asking God's help to rid the countryside of this fearsome monster. When he was ready, he made his way up the mountain to the river's source and the pool carrying three bands of rushes. He stood by the pool and prayed, and didn't the monster rise up and tower over him, for he was thinking that the holy man had been sent as a sacrifice to assuage the fears of the local people.

Murrough didn't disabuse him of the idea and asked the serpent if he could perform a small ritual, an ancient task, before the sacrifice. First, he put the bands on himself and the serpent saw that they were weak. Then he persuaded the serpent to allow the bands to be put on it. But the serpent did not know the power of the holy man's prayer, and right away St Murrough began to pray as he had never prayed before, and the bands became as strong as steel, so strong that the serpent couldn't break them. When the Paiste tried to free itself and couldn't, it cried out in a rage that it had been tricked, but the saint continued to pray in thanksgiving that such a malevolent beast could never break free.

Well, didn't the Paiste try to shout down the saint's prayers, saying that no one or nothing had authority to command it, especially miserable weak humans. You see, it was trying to raise the holy man's temper so he would stop praying and it would be free, but the saint explained that he was only doing the work of God, and as all creatures great and small, and that included the Paiste, were creations of God, the dragon must do as God commanded.

The dragon knew he was beaten, and one ending of the legend tells us that St Murrough banished it downstream to the waters of Lough Foyle forever. If you ever see unusual currents moving along the river it's just the Lig-na-Paiste writhing beneath the surface, still trying to free itself from the bands of steel, but by the grace and wit of St Murrough that won't be till Judgement Day.

If you happen to visit Feeny in County Derry, don't be going around asking where Lig-na-Paiste lies, because the other ending of the story is that the Paiste escaped from the River Foyle and cowers in the pool, still waiting for foolish people to step close.

If you accidently disturb it you're asking for trouble and that's the truth, for it will rise up and strike you stone dead. The people around are adamant that Lig-na-Paiste still lies curled up at the bottom of the pool.

Years ago there was a poor old man who was crippled with rheumatism, and he'd heard that St Murrough had blessed the water in the pool, so he begged his friends to bring him up there. They were very afraid, but the old man begged with tears in his eyes and eventually they gave in. Well, he got himself into a position where he could touch the water, but just as he put his hand in, didn't a big horn rise up out of the water and his friends shouted that it was the Paiste come to devour him. Sure, a miracle did happen, for he leapt to his feet and took off like a hare down that hill and never had an ache or pain again. His friends didn't tell him that they had seen a big branch in the pool and manoeuvred it near him as a joke.

Isn't it strange the way miracles happen?

35

THE WHITE HARE

Away back in the seventeenth century, at the time of the Plantation, the Englishmen who were coerced into coming to Ulster thought that it was a wild and barbarous place. The local people did nothing to put them off their notion, for weren't these foreigners taking the land from them, and if they were a wee bit afraid of them, sure, that suited the natives.

One of the wildest and most mountainous parts where they settled was Muine Móre (the large thicket or hill) now named Moneymore, and these interlopers were known as the gentlemen of the Worshipful Company of Drapers. I suppose that gave them some sort of status, although it didn't make the locals think any more highly of them.

But King James I in London was still having a hard time attracting settlers, so he gave them a sizable parcel of land. But I have to say that the English had no stomach to farm in the middle of this hostile part of the country. Still, they had little choice if they wanted to recoup the money that they paid to London and the coffers of James I. So what could they do? Eventually they settled and made the best of it.

These men, however, were not believers in fairies, ghosts, witches or banshees, for what were they? Only hard-headed businessmen who just wanted to make money. As well as that, didn't they bring their English customs with them, one of these being hunting for pleasure and sure, the locals didn't hold them in any sort of esteem for that. Now, if an Irishman hunts, it's just to get a bite to put on the table, and they couldn't understand why these yokes from England could hunt and kill an animal and then throw it to the hounds to eat. 'What sort of beings were they?' they asked themselves when they heard of some such exploit.

They hunted fox, hare and any other animal they thought of as vermin, and indeed they found that hunting was a bit of distraction from the work and the tensions of living with the native populace. There were plenty of hares running around the fields and the hills so the rich gentlemen of the land seriously took up the sport of hunting the hare. Now, it happens that the Moneymore people were mischievous in their own way, and they let the Englishmen know about one very elusive hare that was all white and seemed to be beyond capture. Sure, the locals knew that the White Hare wasn't really a hare at all but a witch, and didn't the story send them all out on a witch-hunt, only they weren't aware of that. No indeed, but didn't their attempts to capture the White Hare give rise to a lot of laughter around the cottage hearths?

Now, the people of Moneymore also knew that witches have the power to transform themselves into hares and the White Witch Hare was hunted far and wide in County Derry. Because of its magical powers this hare had outrun every hunter up until then, for there was no faster runner in the land. Well, there came a time when those hunters were determined to catch and kill the hare. Sure, wouldn't it be a great feather in their caps, they said, to bring the corpse of the 'most elusive hare in all of Ireland' home. It might also make the antsy natives think twice about crossing the line with the men who caught the White Hare.

The country folk let it be known that the White Hare was in the vicinity and the hunters gathered together at the crossroads with their hounds. They blew their horn and set the hounds off to follow the scent of the hare and didn't the hunters in their fancy riding gear chase after the hounds who were streaking away over the walls? When they reached the open land, sure enough, they saw the flash of white leaping and jumping over and under fences and hawthorn bushes, and the dogs leaping after it in a frenzy of barking.

Then came the hunters, whacking their poor horses' rumps to try to catch up with the hounds, but the hare kept ahead of the hounds and the hounds kept ahead of the hunters and the locals sat drinking and talking about the wild hare chase that the hunters were on.

Sure, they listened until the 'Tally Hos' and horns faded into the distance and then they toasted the White Hare. Out in the countryside, the hunters didn't stop, but jumped over stone walls and hedges, up hills and down glens and the dogs, chased by the thundering hooves of their masters' horses gradually caught up with the White Hare.

And, glory be, didn't one of hounds get close enough to their quarry, and with a blood-curling snarl, manage to bite the White Hare in the thigh? But still she ran on. Sure, it was frightening to hear the hounds yelping behind her, for having had the taste of blood they were in a bigger frenzy. They chased her until she leapt onto the windowsill of a small cottage near the bog and squeezed through the tiny window.

The hounds were yelping and scraping at the door of the cottage and doing their best to get through the narrow window but to no avail. The hunters caught up, for weren't the dogs making a terrible racket, and they had no bother following the commotion. The Master of the Hunt jumped down from his horse and rapped on the door – no answer. He rapped harder, and again, still there was no answer. He pushed the door open and crashed into the cottage.

Well, would you believe what he saw, right in front of his eyes? Not the White Hare, for there was no sign whatsoever of it, but wasn't there an old hag with white straggly hair, sitting by the fire, smoking a long clay pipe? Sure, she just looked at them and spoke not a word but didn't one of the hounds creep over to her and started sniffing at her skirt? And what appeared but blood, seeping through in the exact same spot that the hound had bitten the hare?

As soon as the hunter saw the blood, the old hag jumped up and, as fast as a broom sweeping up hot ash, she was out through that back door, banging it behind her. 'Tis said that no one ever did catch that hare, for sure, everybody, even the gentlemen, believed then that she was just a witch that could change into any living creature.

And oh dear, the farmers had a great fear that she would appear again when May Day came around, and she would make them pay for the hound taking a bite.

For that reason, the wives were up before sunrise on 1 May and the cottage doors were locked, and if any one came in they were give a 'dash' – a sup of the milk from the butter, to make sure that they weren't in league with the fairies or the witches.

That's the legend about the White Hare, and if you ever see that hare, don't give her any reason to turn on you; sure, she could be that self-same witch.

36

THE TALE OF CADHAN'S HOUND

Glenconkeine is the old name of the glen that lies between Carntogher and Slieve Gullion, and there are many legends in this mountainous region associated with mythological hounds and hunting.

In the early seventeenth century, sure, you would see the lords and the gentry out hunting, for it was heavily wooded and there were plenty of places for the deer, rabbits and wild pigs to hide. If you went there now it would hard to believe that it was once forested, for didn't the English cut down all the trees in Ireland to build their huge ships? Anyway, the great woods came in handy when there was any sign of danger from animals, outlaws or the like. The lords could retreat and hide there until the danger passed.

The local people knew that there was a tasty harvest of bilberries each summer on the mountainsides, and celebrations and opportunities were often built around gathering them, including match-making, storytelling and music. Sure, wasn't that why the girls dressed in their best even though they'd be tramping over the heather and the bogs in the hope that they'd meet a nice fellow. Over the months of July and August there were expeditions of happy young girls and boys into the mountains and valleys of County Derry. The parents turned a blind eye when they heard that they were going to pick the berries, for they had no doubt other things went on as well. Sure, many of the fathers and mothers had their first meeting on the mountain on Bilberry Sunday, and why wouldn't they want the same thing for their children?

One of the stories that was told and re-told around the hearths on winter nights was about a hero by the name of Cadhan who went out to pick berries. He found a space amongst the heather loaded with the sweetest berries and as he picked them not all of them went into his bag. He gorged himself on them until he was full to the top of his stomach.

It being a bright sunny Sunday he sat down to rest, but fell asleep and dreamed of heroes and fairies, wee folk and goblins. When he awoke it was near midday and he rushed to get to Sunday Mass, but such was his hurry that he left his bag of fruit behind him. When he came back to that self-same spot on the hillside where he'd fallen asleep and left his bag of fruit, sure, he couldn't find it. It was gone, and in its stead there was a tiny pup, looking up at him with a pathetic look in its big brown eyes. Sure, what could a boy do but bring it home? And that's what he did. He cared for it, but it soon grew to such enormous proportions that he couldn't feed it enough to content it and when rumours began to circulate in the countryside about a monstrous animal devouring the sheep and cattle, Cadhan had his suspicions and locked his hound up in a barn.

The big dog had a cunning brain too and he was able to escape by pawing the earth from under the wall of the barn, and his rampaging continued. Things came to a head when he even began to attack people, for with all his rampaging there was a scarcity of animals. So terrified were people of meeting this monstrous animal that many of them left and crossed the River Bann, hoping that the dog would not follow.

Didn't the tenants go to the lord of the land and beseech him to do something? He wasn't too worried about the poor folk, but since he was losing livestock and his workers were leaving him out of fear, he stirred himself and offered a large reward to the person who would kill the beast and bring its body to him for proof.

Now, Cadhan had lost all love for the hound, so one night he waited on its return and watched it as it entered the barn by the hole. When it was safely asleep he quietly opened up the door and slipped in. Now, he was not afraid that the dog would attack him, because somewhere in the animal's mind it knew that Cadhan was its saviour. Luckily, it did not wake, and Cadhan killed it while it slept. He knew the exact spot to plunge his knife in so that the beast's death would be instantaneous and it would not suffer.

He could see that the blood of the animals the hound had recently slaughtered was hardening on the hound's face, but he did not remove it, knowing that the lord would want proof that this was indeed the feared hound. Gently, he wrapped the animal in a sack and put it over his horse's back to go to the house of the lord to claim the reward offered.

'That's not the animal,' declared the lord. 'It was delivered to me yesterday and the reward was paid out. But,' he said, 'If you leave that creature here I'll have my men dispose of it.'

Cadhan wasn't about to let himself be tricked and he would have none of it, but the lord continued to repudiate Cadhan's claims. He waited until the lord had tied himself in knots with his lies then replied, 'If you do not believe that this is the culprit I shall have to venture to bring its twin to you that you may compare them. But I warn you that he is also a vicious beast and I dare not let him loose.'

The lord handed over the reward forthwith and the country-side settled down. The glen after that was known as Gleann Con Cadhain (The Glen of Cadhan's Hound).

They say that Cadhan built two bonfires to celebrate his victory, and that when the people who had fled across the Bann saw them burning on the hillside they knew it was safe to return. The first one was set alight at the north of the glen, and the other on the slopes of Slieve Gullion, now called Tintagh.

Sometimes on the dark winter nights a strange glow can be seen on Tintagh, and if you listen hard enough you can hear the howl of Cadhan's hound.

37

THE WISH

*This story was one of Sheila Quigley's,
and she told it with great delight.
I hope I have done it justice.*

A long, long time ago, *fadó*, *fadó*, *fadó*, during one of the winters of the great snow, a young man called Barney, his wife Cassie, and his mother lived in a small cottage on the edge of the woods in County Derry. His mother was the bane of his life, for she sat by the fire moaning and complaining most of the time. He was very fortunate that Cassie was very, very patient and looked after the house and his mother, day in and day out, still managing to remain quite cheerful except for one thing. She dearly wanted a baby, for hadn't they been married for seven years? Sure, 'tis no wonder that when no baby had come along she began to despair.

'Twas a bitterly cold day in November and Cassie was hungry. When she had looked that morning, not even a crumb of food lay on the shelf of the dresser. The breadbox was bare and she had no flour in the bin. She couldn't stop herself feeling down and when the tears welled up in her eyes she began to cry softly, for fear of disturbing her mother-in-law, whose sharp hearing made up for her lack of sight. But the old woman heard her and called out.

'What is the matter with you, you miserable child? Is it not bad enough that I am sitting here not able to see? If you were blind you would have something to cry about. You're young, you've your health and strength and my son is the best husband any girl could have.

You don't deserve him so dry up your tears and make me something to eat.'

Cassie wiped her eyes on her apron. The old woman was right. She was more fortunate than most and should count her blessings. But that didn't solve the problem of no food in the house. Instead of crying she would ask Barney if he could hunt a rabbit, bird or anything at all that she could cook.

'What's keeping you, girl? Put some food on the table that I might be able to eat this time, for as sure as God is my judge, your cooking leaves a lot to be desired. If I had my sight I'd show you a thing or two about cooking.'

The girl looked at her mother-in-law and said nothing because she could not trust herself to say something nice. Sure, what could she say to a blind woman who could not see that the cupboard was bare? She went to the barn where her husband was chopping wood.

'Barney,' she called, and her husband put down the axe right away. He could see that Cassie was vexed. 'What's the matter, love?' he asked.

'The scone we had this morning was all we had. What can we do? There not a bite of food in the house and your mother is calling for it. I swear, Barney, I'm ready for the madhouse.'

Barney put his arms around his wife, a bit surprised at her outburst, but knowing in his heart that his auld ma had said something to upset her. She started to cry again.

'Ah, darlin', I'll get my gun and go into the woods to see if I can find something. Take no notice of my ma. Sure, she is not happy unless she can complain.'

Well, Barney went into the house, ignored his mother's call and took heavy coat from the nail on the back of the door. Then he slung his gun over his shoulder, kissed Cassie goodbye and set off, tramping through the heavy snow.

'Barney, be very careful, my love, and come back safely.' Cassie waited in the cold draught of the open door until Barney was out of sight, then she closed the door and went back inside.

Her mother-in-law spoke up right away. 'What are you doing sending that wee boy out on a winter's day like this. Have ye no thought, girl?'

'He's not a wee boy! He's a grown man with responsibilities and if you want to know why he's going out, it's to get some food, for we haven't a crumb in the house.'

'How could ye let things come to such a pass? Couldn't ye have bought flour the last time ye were in the village?' At the old woman's accusatory tone Cassie's temper snapped.

'What with? We have no money. If we had it's food I'd buy, but Barney's too proud to ask you for anything that you keep in that long sock of yours. If you were of a generous mind we'd have food!'

Well, the old woman was so taken aback by Cassie's temper that she fell to muttering to herself and rocking in the chair beside the fire.

'At least you have a warm house!' snapped Cassie, and with that she went into the upper room and slammed the door.

'Things have come to a pretty pass,' she thought, 'when I speak harsh words to a blind woman.' With that, she turned over and fell asleep, for sleep makes one forget about hunger.

Meanwhile, Barney was making his way deeper and deeper into the woods, always on the lookout for any movement or footprints in the snow. It was so silent that he heard his own breathing. He needed to find something quickly, for the winter days were short.

His eyes caught a movement behind a snow-laden bush and quickly he unslung his hunting gun from his shoulder, careful not to make a sound that might scare the animal off. He took aim and fired into the middle of the bush, and right away heard a loud yelp of alarm. No animal ran out but a tiny man, grasping his behind, shot out from the bush.

'Look what ye did!' he cried. 'Ye shot me!'

Barney was too shocked to say or do anything as the little fellow ranted and raged. 'How am I supposed to get home now and me shot in the ass. Eh?'

He turned around, and sure enough, Barney could see that the coat-tail was pierced, but look as hard as he might he could see no sign of blood.

'I don't think you're wounded,' stammered Barney, looking at this wee man who was less than twelve inches high.

'No thanks to ye. Only for me two fleet feet I'd be lying there dead. What ails ye anyway?' said the leprechaun, for that's what he was.

'We've no food in the house, not a bite, and I thought you were a rabbit or a pheasant. That's why I shot. I'm very sorry,' said Barney, 'I meant you no harm.'

'Ah, well, if ye give me a shoulder home, I'll see that ye get something.' With that, the wee man skedaddled over to Barney and took a running jump onto his shoulder.

'That way,' ordered the leprechaun, pointing even deeper into the woods.

'I don't know these parts so you better direct me,' said Barney, and so he did. To Barney it seemed that he had walked miles, and he was a bit afraid of not getting home before night fell.

'Don't be worrying about that,' said the wee man, reading Barney's mind. 'Ye'll be home quicker than two daisies wantin' their heads. Any road, we're here. Ye can let me down now.'

Right in front of Barney was a huge oak tree, and only if you looked closely, which Barney did, could you see that there was a tiny door above the first branch.

'Ye can pop me up there,' said the leprechaun, 'and I thank ye kindly. An' I can tell ye now,' said he in a conspiratorial whisper, 'sure I wasn't shot at all, at all.' With that he laughed, and sure, what could Barney do but join in the laughter.

The leprechaun motioned him closer, and when Barney was within earshot of the whisper the wee man said, 'I'll give you one wish for your trouble, but mind ye have to take it afore noon tomorrow or you lose it. But be careful what ye wish for, because I can tell ye now that ye'll have some bother.'

Barney wasn't too sure that the leprechaun was telling the truth or if it was just another yarn like him being shot when he wasn't.

'Aye,' said the wee man, ''tis the truth I'm telling ye, and to prove it; look behind this tree and ye'll get a brace of pheasants. Go on.'

Barney walked behind the tree, and true to the leprechaun's word there was a magnificent brace of pheasants. He unhooked them and went back to thank the wee man, but there was no one there.

He shook his head in wonder, and when he opened his eyes, where was he but at his own front door?

Now if that wasn't magic, what was?

He left the pheasants outside for the moment, pushed open the door and went in. His mother was sitting at the fire, rocking in the chair.

'Where's Cassie?' he asked.

'Don't ask me. She went off to bed in a flounce and I haven't seen her since. You're back very early so ye couldn't have caught anything.'

Barney looked at the wag-at-the-wall clock and saw that only a half hour had elapsed since he left the farm. Cassie must have heard the talking and came out of the bedroom.

'Aw, Barney,' she cried, 'I was afraid you'd get lost. Never mind the food, sure we'll get something tomorrow.'

Barney smiled and went outside. When he entered again he had the brace of pheasants in his hand. Cassie whooped with joy and threw herself into his arms.

'How did you manage that in such a short time?'

Barney began to relate his adventure, and when he finished he added, 'I have one wish to make before noon tomorrow and guess what I'm going to wish for? A big bag of gold so we can build a new cottage with a separate room for ma, and we can buy every-thing we want and we'll never go hungry again.' He gave a smile of self-satisfaction, hooked his thumbs into his trouser braces and rocked backwards and forwards on his heels.

'Ye what!' screeched his mother, 'ye'd wish for money when here I am, sitting and every day as black as the last and ye wouldn't wish for me to see again. A fine son ye are, by God!'

Cassie looked at him sadly, 'What about a baby. Would you not wish for a baby that I could hold in my arms and sing a lullaby to? Sure, you know how much I've been longing for that.'

Barney's self-satisfaction disappeared and he remembered the words of the leprechaun that he'd have some bother with the wish.

'We'll cook up a nice bird now and then I'll sleep on it.' After that Barney would not be drawn on what wish he would make, for truth be told, he had no idea himself and it was a quandary for him.

That night he tossed and turned and beside him Cassie got very little sleep. Came the morning he was no closer to making a decision, but with only half an hour to noon the solution hit him like a thunderbolt. He called his wife in and the two of them stood beside his mother.

'Now', he said, 'before I make my wish. I want the two of to agree that I've made the right decision.'

'Sure I can't do that if I don't know what it is!' exclaimed his mother.

He looked at his wife and she nodded 'Yes.'

'So Ma, I'm trying to be fair and I never want to hear a sour word out of your mouth again. You'll just have to trust me on this.' He squeezed her shoulder and she gave her 'Yes.'

'Now that that's settled, my wish is this.' He closed his eyes and spoke slowly, 'I wish that my mother could watch my wife rocking our baby in a golden cradle.'

And at the stroke of twelve noon, would you believe that it all came to pass.

Fadó, long ago.

38

THE LOOKING GLASS

Now, this story goes away way back to the times when the poor tenant farmers had little or nothing and not many of them had ever seen a mirror, and ye can ask yourself why would any of them want a mirror anyway?

Well, to get on with the story, there was a man called Dinny who lived with his wife of fifty years in a wee farm away out on the far side of Derry. Sure Dinny and Brigid were innocent folk, just wee farmers who worked hard. But there was one day in the year that Brigid was glad to be on her own and that was the day that Dinny went to the fair in Derry. Now, he didn't go just to sell the donkey that was as lazy as sin, naw, he went for a bit of *craic* and chat with other farmers that he never saw from one six months till the next. Sure, it was all the better if that happened to be in a pub, because that was the one place you could be guaranteed to get away from the women.

Brigid wasn't averse to him going; sure, didn't she always press his Sunday suit for him to wear, and polish up his boots, and put a decent white collar on his shirt with a mother-of-pearl stud? When the cock crowed on the May morning Brigid patted him on the back and sent him off, knowing it would take a good while to walk the length of Derry.

Ye see, Brigid couldn't wait to get him out of the house, for she had a secret vice that she never wanted Dinny to know about. Didn't she like to have a read of a wee romantic story in the book that her sister Ellen had sent her from New York? She knew Dinny would think it a load of nonsense if he could see it, for 'twas more the pity that Dinny hadn't a romantic bone in his body, God be good to him. One time she asked him to bring her a bunch of flowers from the fair, because that's what the hero in the book did, and what did Dinny say?

'What good is flowers? Sure, ye can't eat them!' and that was that. Poor Brigid had to content herself that the only romance she was ever going to get was from a book.

As soon as Dinny turned the bend in the road and the wee donkey trotting beside him, Brigid pulled the book out from under the mattress, cut a big slice of soda bread, and made a cup of tea for herself, and she was ready to sit down and read it, for she'd been waiting for six months to get on with the story. She wasn't a fast reader, mind you, for she only got the chance when Dinny left for the fair day but sure, poor Dinny didn't know the pleasure of it, for he couldn't read. At school he never got past the first reader, and that was because his da needed him on the farm.

Anyway, she put a cushion on top of the turf basket and stretched out her legs, and oh boy, she was as happy as the day was long. Dinny wouldn't be home for another six hours or so, maybe more if he was drunk, and she might even manage to finish the story.

Dinny marched sprightly along and swung his blackthorn stick around. Sure, it was great to be out in the fresh air of the first day of May. Just to be on the safe side of the fairies, he called out 'White Rabbit,' three times for luck, in the firm belief that nothing would ail him for the day.

Man sir, when he reached Derry it was buzzing like a hive of bees. He heard a voice calling and looked around, and there was Paddy McLaughlin, a fellow he was used to seeing on these occasions.

'Oi, Dinny. 'Tis good tae see ye, sir. Are ye havin' wan?' said he, nodding in the direction of the pub.

'I am so,' said Dinny and they walked together down Shipquay Street, the wee donkey trotting beside them.

'If ye are going to sell that wee donkey, I have a mind to buy it,' said Paddy.

''Six bob and it's yours,' said Dinny.

'Five,' said Paddy.

'Right ye are,' answered Dinny. The two men spit on their hands and shook, to seal the bargain.

Now, didn't Dinny spend most of the money on the drink, and at six o'clock he was staggering out of the pub with just a ween o' ha'pence in his pocket. On the way out of the town he saw a man selling all sorts of fripperies on a stall and he wove his way over. He was thinking that Brigid might be vexed that he'd spent so much money, and if he bought her a wee something he could say it cost more. Satisfied with his logic he rummaged around and picked up a wee brooch.

'How much,' he asked the pedlar,

'Thru'pence,' said he, eyeing Dinny as a soft touch. Dinny left it down as if he was scalded and picked up a wee looking glass, holding it up close.

'Oh my God,' said he to the man, 'Where did you get that?'

And the man said back to him, 'Why? D'ye want to buy it?'

'Course, I do,' said Dinny, 'Sure that's a picture of my father. How much d'ye want for it?'

'One and six,' said the pedlar. Dinny shook his head. Brigid's present was going to have to go by the by, for he hadn't enough money left. God curse the drink for using it up!

The pedlar measured him up again. Better a sale than none at this time of day. 'I'll give you the two for one and six,' he said, and Dinny slapped his thigh.

'Done,' said he and took the two things and put Brigid's brooch in his pocket. Well, as he walked along the road he stopped every now and then and took the mirror out of his pocket. And sure he nearly had tears in his eyes. 'Ah, well,' said he, 'wasn't my father the fine-looking man.'

Now then, when he got home, he hung his coat on the nail at the back of the door but Brigid, seeing his flushed cheeks and the way he nearly tripped over on the step coming in, scolded him.

'It's the only suit you have, here, I'll hang it up for you.'

'Naw, don't bother,' said he, for I have a wee present for ye.' And he put his hand into his pocket and brought out the brooch. He never took out the looking glass for Brigid and his da never got on at all.

Heis da had always thought her too uppity and sure, she wouldn't want to know that he spent money on a picture of his father.

'You've brought me a present?' said Brigid in shock, for Dinny had never bought her one before. He handed her the brooch and she nearly threw her arms around him she was that pleased. Dinny saw the light in her eyes and stepped back, afeard of what she would do. Sure, she pinned the brooch on her apron and smiled, and then hung the kettle on the crook over the fire.

Well, she forgot about her vexation until she saw Dinny going to his coat pocket at every opportunity, taking something out and smiling to himself. She waited till he went to bed, for after a day's drinking he was always tired. She shut the bedroom door and went to his coat and took the looking glass out of his pocket.

'Oh, Holy Mary, what's my Dinny doing carrying a picture of a woman round in his pocket? And I wouldn't mind but she's the dourest looking woman I ever saw in my life.' She shoved the mirror back in his coat pocket and went to bed. Sure, she tossed and turned that night, thinking that 'twas no wonder Dinny bought her a brooch for 'twas a guilty conscience he had.

The next day, when he started gleaking in his pocket at all sorts of times that morning she couldn't stick it for one more minute.

'Come 'ere, you,' she said, 'What are you doing going round with a picture of a woman in your pocket?'

'What are ye talking about, Brigid? Sure, that's a picture of me da,' he said.

'Well,' she said, 'I never saw your da wae straggly hair like that nor teeth missing, like I saw on that auld dame last night! Aye, you crafty wee skitter ye, I knew you had something to hide when you brought me home a brooch, for never in your life did you buy me anything.'

'What are ye on about, Brigid? I bought that and the wee picture of me da from the pedlar in Derry.'

'That's no picture of your da, that's a picture of a woman.'

'Don't be daft, Brigid, sure that's me da and he's a fine-looking man, so he is.'

'I'm telling you now, Dinny McCool, you'll hear more about this for I'm not satisfied, no, indeed I'm not!'

Well, the next day, when he was out on the hill with the sheep, didn't Brigid get onto her bicycle and cycle to the parochial house, for she wanted the priest to have a word with Dinny. When he opened the door she started bawling, even before she had a word out.

'Come in, woman dear. What's the matter?' said the priest, ushering her in.

'Aw Father, me heart's breaking, so it is. That blaggard of a man of mine is going around with a picture of a woman in his pocket. And if she was a good-looking woman, it wouldn't be so bad, but she's the worst-looking woman I ever set eyes on.'

Said the priest, 'Now settle yourself, Brigid, there must be some explanation.'

'Explanation, my eye,' answered Brigid, 'Sure, I saw her picture myself, and there she was staring out of the picture, as bold as brass, and just as ugly.'

'Now, Brigid, listen to me an' this is what you'll do. You go on home and keep your own counsel, say nothing to Dinny, but I'll go over tonight and sort things out. Don't fret yourself till I see Dinny. There's a good woman.' And he patted her on the back and walked her to the door. Once he shut it he sighed, thinking that the life of a parish priest was not an easy one.

That night Brigid sat at the table and not a sound came out of her. Dinny kept looking, for that wasn't Brigid's form at all, at all.

'Is there something ailing ye, Brigid?' he asked, but Brigid just cleared away the dinner dishes and sat down with her knitting at the fire. There came a knock on the door and Dinny opened it.

'Well, come on in, Father. Sure, it's grand to see ye. Brigid, it's the priest come to visit.'

Brigid rose, 'What brings you out this way tonight, Father? Sure, I haven't seen you for a long while,' she said, all innocent-like.

'Ach, I was just passing this way and saw the light,' said the priest, thinking to himself that women were crafty two-faced creatures.

'I'm going out to shut the byre, Father, but make yourself comfortable,' said Dinny reaching for his coat behind the door.

'Hold on a wee minute, Dinny for I want to have a few words with you.'

'Aye, sure, do ye want a wee job on the parochial house or something?'

'No,' answered the priest, 'it's a bit more serious, Dinny, and what I want is a straight answer from you. Are you carrying a picture of a woman around in your pocket?'

'Ach, Father, I know now what you're here for, that story came from Brigid. There's no truth in it, Father, for I can tell you now that it's a picture of my own father I have in my pocket, and a fine looking man he was an all.'

Brigid looked askance at Dinny, then turned to the priest. 'Father, don't you be listening to him, for it's the picture of a woman he has in his pocket and a rough-looking hussy she is too.'

'Hush Brigid,' said the priest, holding up his hand. 'We'll settle this once and for all. Dinny, give me that picture out of your pocket right now.'

'Right ye are, Father,' he said and plucked the mirror from his pocket, 'There ye are.' And he handed it to the parish priest.

Then the priest looked at it and began to laugh. 'Well,' he said, 'aren't you the two right eejits? Sure, isn't that the parish priest who was here before me!'

I heard this story from Aussie Bryson, a great storyteller from Donegal. He says that he heard it from some else, who heard it from someone else etc.

39

WHAT YOU WANT IS
NOT WHAT YOU NEED

*The following story could well be one for these times in
Ireland when differences are being challenged and solved.*

It was a tough time, sure enough, for farmers during and
after the Plantation of Ulster. They were used to reaping a
rich harvest on the low-lying fertile plain of Magilligan and
along the banks of the Foyle estuary. Where the Foyle, Bann
and Faughan rivers and their tributaries ran on the way to the
sea there was always enough arable land along their banks to
harvest a good crop.

Now, the background to the next story goes back to 'owner-
ship' and the fierce pride that people have in what they own, be
it house, land or animals. Maybe it's even more pronounced in
Ulster people who lost their lands, and that history is still stuck in
their minds. As the old expression says – 'What I have I hold!' So,
having lost land once before in the Plantation, they were loth to
lose it or their valuables or 'chattels' ever again.

Sure, we all know that the London Guilds didn't want to
come here at all and Parliament had to 'coerce' them into colo-
nising Ulster west of the River Bann. Weren't they heart-scared
of doing that because it was the land of the possessive and fero-
cious O'Cahan clan. The native Irish objected to their lands being
given to the English Crown and there were some terrible atrocities

when they tried to reclaim it. There was a bit of disarray amongst the settlers when the king of England was executed and the Irish took advantage, rising in rebellion. Having terrible Irish tempers, they destroyed nearly every settlement, except for Coleraine and Londonderry, which were too well fortified.

So you see, with all that sort of history rattling in the background it's easy to see that the old blood about possession can be stirred up and no one will give an inch. Sure, even best friends and families can fall out over the head of a wee thing like a lamb.

Ned lived out in the countryside, halfway up a hill on a wee farm. He scratched a living from the poor land, enough to feed his wife and weans. Mary, his wife, was long gone to her rest and his family were scattered all over the world, since there wasn't much of a future for them at home. Ned was contented enough, for hadn't he a cow and a wee flock of sheep.

His best friend James was also his closest neighbour. They had grown old together and shared many a joy and sorrow and sure, being on their own, all they had left was each other. But this story was a silly argument over a stray lamb that neither one of them even needed. Now, the lamb was on James's land and he claimed it but Ned was adamant that it was his, for wasn't the lamb crying to get back to its mother, and the ewe was equally distressed.

'It's mine,' shouted Ned.

'I say it belongs to me,' shouted James back. And so it went on until they both said things they would regret, for a bad temper knows no restraint on the tongue.

Aw, they were stubborn men and neither would give in, but, being old, they didn't come to blows, ah no, they just stopped shouting at each other and stomped off to their own houses and slammed the doors shut.

A month passed and not a word was said between them. Old Ned was feeling lonely but still angry, for he was of a mind that James was in the wrong. One morning he heard a knock, sort of gentle-like, on his door. He was surprised, for very few people came to call on him. When he opened the door there was a young man standing on the flagstone outside. He introduced himself as a carpenter who travelled around the country doing jobs here and there. Ned could see that he looked fairly respectable and had a wooden toolbox at his feet. He had a kind smile and two twinkling eyes and Ned felt right at ease with him.

'I'm looking for work,' said the young man 'and if you have any jobs that need doing, I'd be happy to help you out.'

Ned rubbed his hand over his chin and answered, 'As a matter of fact, aye, I have a job you could do. D'ye see that house across the hill there, that's my neighbour's house. And d'ye see that wee burn (stream) running along there, well, that's our property line and that burn wasn't there last week. He just did that to spite me. I watched him digging that ditch along there, and he diverted the burn from the upper pool and flooded it right down that property line. So now we've got a stream of water to separate us.'

The young man gazed at the stream, then at Ned's face, and he could read the frustration there. 'I understand,' said he, 'What do you want me to do?'

'I'm so mad at him. I've got wood and all you need over there in my barn, enough to build a fence. I want you to build a tall fence, all along that burn, and then I won't even have to see his house again, for he has my heart scalded. That'll teach him.'

The carpenter smiled and lifted his toolbox. 'I'll do a good job for you, Ned.'

'Right-io,' said Ned, 'I have to go to the town to get some stuff so ye'll be on your own. Just make yourself something to eat when you want. The door's open.' And with that he set off on his donkey and cart to Derry.

The carpenter carried the wood he needed to the stream and then started to work. He worked all day without a break, not even for lunch, measuring, sawing and nailing the wood into place. With the setting of the sun he gathered his tools, cleaned them and put them away, well satisfied with his work. Just then, old Ned returned and when he saw the job that the carpenter had done, he couldn't speak, for it wasn't the high fence that he had asked for, but a beautiful footbridge with carved handrails reaching from Ned's side of the stream to the other.

Old James came walking across the field and crossed the bridge with his hand stuck out. Ned took it and held on.

'I'm sorry about our misunderstanding, Ned. That lamb is yours. I don't know what got into me. I just want us to go on being good friends, for it's lonely up here with you and me not speaking. When I saw the bridge I said to myself, that's just the wee push I needed to come on over here.'

'Na, you keep the lamb, James. I want us to be friends too. But the bridge was this young fellow's idea.' Ned turned and the carpenter was hoisting the toolbox onto his shoulder ready to leave.

'Hold on,' said Ned, 'What do I owe you.'

'You've already paid me,' he said, looking at the clasped hands.

'Well, young fellow,' said James. 'Me and Ned here could keep you busy for weeks, what with all the wee jobs around the farms.'

The carpenter smiled and said, 'I'd like to stay, James, but I can't. I have more bridges to build.' And with that he walked on down the road, whistling a happy tune.

This tales is one of those that were brought to America by emigrants. I heard it when I was young and, once, on an Arts Council Storytelling visit on the west coast I heard a similar one told. It is obviously one that has a message for most people.

BIBLIOGRAPHY &
FURTHER READING

Audley, B., 'The Provenance of the Londonderry Air', *Journal of the Royal Musical Association* (2000) Vol. 125(2), pp.205-247

Journal of the Irish Folk Song Society (October 1912.) Vol. 12

Royal Society of Antiquaries of Ireland (1903)

CBS souvenir prospectus and programme (Cristian Brothers Press; Derry, *c*. 1928)

Historical Gleanings from County Derry and some from Fermanagh (Monument Press Dublin, 1955)

Davis, C., *Celtic Illumination* (Gill & McMillan; Dublin, 2001)

Davis, C. & James, D., *The Celtic Image* (Cassell & Co., 2000)

Day & McWilliams (eds), *OS Memoirs of Ireland, Parishes C. Londonderry IX, 1832-38*, Vol. 28 (Inst. Irish Studies QUB)

Dunlop, E., *Tales of Columba* (Poolbeg, 1992)

Foster, J.C., *Ulster Folklore* (HR Carter Pub.; Belfast, 1951)

Gregory, Lady, *Lady Gregory's Complete Irish Mythology* (Bounty Books; London, 2004)

Heaney, M., *Over Nine Waves* (Faber & Faber; London, 1994)

McCormack, K., *Ken McCormack's Derry* (Londubh Books; Dublin, 2010)

McFadden, V., *Island City* (Lederg History Press; Moville, 1982)

McMahon, S., *A Derry Anthology* (Blackstaff Press; Belfast, 2002)

M'Keefry, Revd J., 'The County Derry Rapparee' *The Journal of the Royal Society of Antiquaries of Ireland*, Series 5, Vol. XII (1902), pp. 232-238

∽

Otway, C., *Sketches in the North and South of Ireland* (W. Curry Jnr, 1827)

Smith, D., *A Guide to Irish Mythology* (Irish Academic Press, 1988)

FURTHER READING

Bonner, B., *Where Aileach Guards* (Foilseacháin Náisiúnta Teo.; Dublin, 1974)

Bratton, Robert, *Round the Turf Fire* (Talbot Press; Dublin, 1931)

Byrne, P.F., *Tales of the Banshee* (Mercier; Cork, 1987)

Colby, Col. R.E., *Ordnance Survey of the County of Londonderry* (Hodges & Smith; Dublin, 1837)

Coghlan, R., *A Dictionary of Irish Myth and Legend* (Donard Pub. Company, 1979)

Croker T.C., *Irish Fairy Legends* (Dover Publications, NY, 2008)

Curran, Bob., *Banshees, Beasts and Brides from the Sea* (Appletree Press, 1996)

Joyce, P.W., *Old Celtic Romances* (Wordsworth Editions, 2000)

McClintock, C., *Columba, The Last Irish Druid* (Aesun Publishing, 2012)

McMahon, S. (ed.), *A History of County Derry* (Gill & McMillan; Dublin, 2004)

Martin, Sam, *Mummers* (Dolmen Press Ltd; Dublin, 1964)

Mitchell, B., *On the Banks of the Foyle* (Friar's Bush Press; Belfast, 1999)

O'Faolain, E., *Irish Sagas and Folk Tales* (Poolbeg, 1986)

Ulster Architectural Heritage Society, *In and Near the City of Derry* (UAHS, 1970)

Wilde, W.R., *Irish Popular Superstitions* (Irish University Press; Shannon, 1852)

Yeats, W.B., Compilation. *Fairy and Folk Tales of Ireland* (Bounty Books; London, 2004)

NEWSPAPERS

Derry Journal
Londonderry Sentinel
Coleraine Chronicle

WEBSITES

www.nooseornecklace.com
www.limavady.gov.uk